ONE HUNDRED SECRETS

AN ASPEN COVE SMALL TOWN ROMANCE

KELLY COLLINS

BOOK NOOK PRESS

CHAPTER ONE

It was every girl's dream wedding, from the dress to the stretch limousine. Goldie Sutherland sipped her champagne and looked out the window as the forest's snow-capped trees stared down on her like disapproving giants.

"Stop judging," she said out loud.

"Excuse me, ma'am." The limo driver glanced at her in the rearview mirror. "Did you need something?"

Goldie pasted on her social smile. The same smile she'd been trained to perfect since she was a child.

"No, just thinking out loud."

"No problem. Would you like me to raise the

privacy screen so you can think without interruption?"

Did she? She'd spent most of her life alone, and it was nice that another human was only several feet away from her and engaged, if only because he was paid.

"Whatever you're most comfortable with," she replied.

The window came up to lock her in solitary confinement. Funny how a life built around social media could be so lonely.

The long tulle skirt of her wedding dress puddled at her feet. It was right out of a fairytale. Silk bodice with pearl buttons. A cinched waist that led to yards and yards of tulle embellished with tiny handsewn sequins and pearls. Even the shoes were special, with acrylic heels and embroidered lace and Swarovski crystal insets. The final touch was a white faux fur shawl that hung perfectly around her shoulders to protect her from the winter's chill.

She opened her clutch and pulled out her phone. There were several missed texts from Sebastian, her groom. The first was all lower case, *call me*. The second threw in some caps, *Call Me, right away*. The last message was like a scream *CALL ME NOW!!!!!*

She rolled her eyes and dialed. Sebastian was

always a drama king. Like her, he was a social influencer, which in plain English meant they were great at getting people to buy crap they didn't need.

"Finally," Sebastian yelled.

Goldie held the phone from her ear. "What the hell is the matter? You're on your way, right?"

There was a pause that didn't sit right in her gut. Nothing with Sebastian went in slow motion. He was a full steam ahead kind of guy, which made him the perfect temporary husband.

"We've got a problem."

She sat up, nearly tipping over her champagne. Her fingers gripped tightly to the stem. "There's no room for problems. Everything is set to the minute."

"You'll need a new plan."

Goldie's mind reeled. "What part of the plan?"

"The whole thing."

She cocked her head and replayed his words. "The whole thing? Like as in you'll be late? Your tux doesn't fit? You woke up and you're bald? What part of the plan is failing?"

Sebastian sighed. "The part where my girlfriend said if I marry you, she's leaving me."

"What?" The champagne glass tumbled from her shaking fingers and landed on the carpet in front of her, barely missing the skirt of her gown. "We went over this a thousand times. It's a temporary marriage. The publicity will do you good and save my career."

She'd been losing her following steadily for the last year. Her millions of followers had dwindled down to a few hundred thousand, then tens of thousands and was still heading south. She was a sinking ship. This entire secret wedding hoax was a last-ditch effort to pull in a broader audience. It was her life preserver and now there was a hole in her plan.

Nancy, her publicist, had put the whole thing in motion six months ago. Goldie's Secret Groom had boosted her ratings and pulled in a lot of sponsorships. It had become a modern-day Where's Waldo in the social scene, but without a groom, she was screwed.

"Chloe said if I married you today, she'd leave me. She doesn't want to marry a divorcé and since she's Catholic she doesn't want to have to deal with the whole Vatican annulment thing when we finally get married."

Goldie grew dizzy. She gripped the door for stability. "But you were going to use the additional sponsorship money to help pay for your real wedding. I don't understand what went wrong." She watched the trees whiz by as the driver raced toward their secret destination. A place chosen for its small-town appeal and beautiful landscape. A place that would be missing an important component of her plan—a groom. A place called Aspen Cove.

Nancy had some connection to the popstar Indigo, who'd told her Hope Park would be a great place to take photos.

"You can't call me on the morning of our wedding and tell me you're not showing. I need a damn groom, or I'm ruined."

She'd known Sebastian through a friend of a friend, which meant he wasn't a friend at all. Social influencers had collaborators, not friends. It was why she sat in a limousine alone. No family. No bridesmaids. No support.

The term influencer was used loosely and meant she could help push an agenda, show up for a mutually advantageous event, or ride the coattails of a bigger brand. That brand had been her for years, but sadly she was an aging influencer, and she could only remain twenty-six for several years before people took notice.

"I'm sorry, Goldie, but in all honesty, this was always about you and not me. Chloe pointed out that like real stars, your light died years ago and we're just seeing the last tiny flicker fade to darkness."

"Rude. I'm not a has-been." She'd been telling herself that for a while. "I'm in a lull."

Sebastian chuckled. "You're in denial. You know once you hit thirty, you're on the road to retirement."

"If you don't stop, I swear I'll hunt you down and you'll never hit thirty. Besides, I'm twenty-six."

He huffed, "Fine, you're twenty-six but you're on your eighth anniversary of that birthday."

Her mouth dropped open. "I'm not thirty-four."

"And you're not twenty-six either. Isn't it time you were honest with yourself?"

"Says the guy who has his six-pack sprayed on weekly. Give me a break. No one in this business is honest."

Sebastian let out a long exhale. "It's all smoke and mirrors. I get it, but I can't lie about who I love, or I'll lose her. I'm not coming. That's all you need to know."

A tear slipped from her eye. She dabbed a finger against her cheek so as not to disturb her makeup but still swipe the tear aside.

"What the hell am I going to do now? Everyone will want their product or money back."

Again, the silence ate up the space around her.

"I'd suggest one of two things. You run and hide, or you find another groom immediately."

The end of his call delivered the blow of finality. She was alone and in big trouble.

She moved her fingers across the screen of her phone. She hoped Nancy would answer, but she didn't.

The limousine slowed as they entered the town of Aspen Cove.

Out the window, she could see the photographer setting up his tripod in front of the gazebo. The only saving grace was the wedding was secret, so there weren't any paparazzi or fans. Then again, there hadn't been any of those in a long time.

Sebastian was right, she was old and over. How was it possible that at thirty-two she was washed up?

The limousine pulled to the curb and the privacy window rolled down.

"Ms. Sutherland, we've reached your destination. Would you like to exit the car?"

"No, I'll need a few minutes."

"Very well. You can control the privacy screen too. Let me know when you're ready." It slid back into place, leaving her alone to deal with her abandonment.

Why was she always alone? Her mother's voice echoed in her head. "In this business, you can only count on you. The other bastards will sell your soul to the devil to get a step ahead." Liza Sutherland had been an iconic movie star in her day. She wasn't a great mother, but she sure could say her lines. At the end of her heyday, she'd brought her daughter into the business. More like sold Goldie's soul to the devil when she used her to get a gig called "Growing Up with Goldie" which was one of the first reality television series aired. Her life was on display for the entire world to see. All the good, the bad, and the ugly—mostly the ugly because everyone loved a train wreck. The series ended in much the same way as Goldie's life was going today—crash and burn.

The network abandoned them, telling her mother the public had lost interest and had out-grown her. How sad it was to watch her mom try to claw her way to the top again only to lose her life in what should have been a quick nip and tuck for a new series about aging starlets. Liza Sutherland was happy to be on the show, but there was no way she'd ever appear to age.

Goldie scrubbed her hands over her face, not

caring if her false lashes fell off or her sponsored siren red lipstick smudged. She needed a plan and she needed one now.

The tulle of the dress gathered around her legs, the rough material making her skin itch and crawl. How was it this dress cost over twenty thousand dollars when her cotton nightshirt was far more comfortable? The damn shoes on her feet had rubbed her heels raw and she hadn't even taken a step. The crystal tiara poked into the beads of her extensions.

Her life was a mess, spiraling out of control for the last year. Without a groom, she'd be homeless within a month, maybe sooner.

"That's it." She pulled out her mirror from her clutch and checked her makeup. Thankfully everything was long wear and had fared well. She touched up the lipstick, powdered her nose and checked her wallet for cash. "I need a groom, which means I may have to pay for one."

She had five hundred dollars. It was the last of her resources. The last of any money she had to her name. She couldn't imagine the quality of groom she could purchase with so little, but hell if she wouldn't try.

Her bank account was empty and would only plump up when the sponsors' products were mentioned and seen in her wedding pictures. "Love Goldie's lipstick, click here." Each purchase put a little cash in her account. That was the way of her job. She got nothing if people weren't interested. No one would tune in if her groom wasn't present.

She lowered the privacy screen. "I need you to pull into town so I can get something I need."

"Yes, ma'am. Anywhere in particular?"

"Wherever you think I'd find the most people."

She shuddered to think about what kind of man she'd have to marry to put ramen in her cupboard for the week. Her only alternative was to find another job, but that was impossible because her age was not her only secret.

The limousine moved down the street until they were parked in front of a place named Maisey's Diner.

It took a great deal of self-talk to gear her up for the task at hand. The driver stood by her door. The rule was when she was ready for her big reveal, she would knock on the window. This was not the fake wedding day she had in mind.

She took a deep breath and tapped the glass.

He opened the door and she ducked so she wouldn't take off her tiara or her fake hair. She practically rolled out of the back seat and hopped to her feet, a cloud of tulle floating around her. Heads turned as she made her way inside.

A bell above the door rang. She walked in, looked around and breathed in the smell of bacon and fresh coffee.

It was a fifties diner from its red upholstered booths to its checkerboard floor tile.

Heads rose at her entrance. It wasn't every day a bride strolled into the local greasy spoon. In the corner sat an older man who peeked over his newspaper. He raised a bushy white brow before ducking back behind the news.

Across the room appeared to be a classroom of children or a family who didn't know birth control existed. The table to her left had a couple cooing over their newborn and another woman looking on as if she expected something unusual to happen.

Goldie refused to disappoint. The only wrench in her plan was the lack of single males seated in the establishment. Outside of the old geezer in the corner, there was one other man. On closer inspection, he was a cross between a grizzly bear and a convict, but he was alone and didn't wear a ring. In her book, that meant he was fair game.

Tailored suits and ties were more her type. She didn't mind a man that beat her to the mirror in the morning. It was part and parcel of her way of life. But desperate times called for desperate measures, and if Mr. Mountain Man said yes, she'd say I do in a second flat.

Pulling back her shoulders, she took the five hundred-dollar bills from her clutch and held them in the air.

"I need a groom, and I need one now." She stared straight at the only single man under seventy and over twenty. "What about you?"

CHAPTER TWO

Tilden Cool looked up at Wedding Dress Barbie and laughed. He was no Ken.

"Excuse me?" He rubbed his hand over his bearded face thinking she was a mirage of sorts. A damn nightmare maybe.

The woman rushed toward him with her skirt rustling behind her. She pulled out the chair across from him and plunked herself down. The swirl of white material floated around her like thick fog. Only the air that rushed forward didn't shout, "All is sunny." It screamed, "Storm brewing, take cover."

Her tiny little hand thrust forward until it hovered in front of him. "My name is Goldie Sutherland, and this is your lucky day." Her teeth were perfect, her lips as red and shiny as a candy-coated apple. On a different day, he might have considered licking them to see if they were as sweet as they looked, but he was a logical thinker and women in wedding dresses looking for grooms spelled trouble.

He stared down at her hand and offered his, which completely engulfed hers. That wasn't a surprise, really. He'd never been considered a small man. Add to that his quiet demeanor and his air of mystery, and most people left him alone. He liked his life that way. People had a way of complicating things that should be simple.

"I'm Tilden Cool." He didn't speak much so it often shocked him how deep his voice was.

Her eyes grew wide. "Your name is Tilden?"

"Last time I checked my driver's license, that's what it said." He gathered his papers and pushed them aside. He often spent his time at this table in the diner. It was a quiet place where he could balance his checkbook. Research for authors and edit their work. Outside of delivering firewood for Zachariah, he didn't have many ways to earn a living. The few dollars he earned for each delivery didn't go far.

"Tilden Cool." She said his name like she was tasting it. "That's an interesting name." She looked down at his papers. His truck payment was at the top of the pile. "Bills, they're evil."

His brows lifted. "Is there something you needed from me, Goldie?"

She pulled a plump red lip between her teeth. When it popped free, she turned on her hundred-watt smile. "Well, yes, there is. I'm glad you asked." She looked around the diner for a second and then tucked the billowing material under her thighs. "I think you and I could help each other." She raised her left hand to show the crumpled hundred-dollar bills in her grasp.

"What did that money do to compel you to choke it to death?"

She giggled. It was a sweet sound.

He stared into eyes that weren't brown per se, but more of a cognac color or a melted caramel. Her blonde hair was streaked with different hues, from straw to coffee latte.

"I'm in a bind." She leaned into the center of the table. "I'm supposed to be married in fifteen minutes, but my groom is missing."

He nodded his head. "Problematic."

"I'll say." She flattened the bills onto the table, pushing the creases to the sides with trembling fingers. "I hoped I could pay you to stand in for him."

"Like a surrogate?" His voice was louder and

bolder than he intended. His eyes traveled to Thomas and Eden Cross, who'd had their own surrogate crisis. The woman sitting with them was her sister, who could also be considered the devil incarnate if early stories rang true. Seeing her now smiling at their baby, she didn't appear so evil, but then again, everything could be dressed up to look like something else. He was sitting across from a bride who had no groom.

"Yes, I guess. I need someone to marry me now. I need *you* to marry me now."

Tilden pushed his chair back a few inches. Was it fight or flight, or maybe the air was getting thin in the diner? "You what?"

Maisey walked over with a pot of coffee in one hand and a cup in the other. "Would you like some?" Since he had a cup already, she was no doubt speaking to Goldie.

"No, I think she's leaving." He picked up his papers and shoved them into a nearby folder. "I'm leaving too. Can I get my check?"

"I'd love a cup, please." She reached over and put her hand on his. "Hear me out."

"No one here is selling what you're looking for."

Maisey looked between them. "We got cakes and eggs and the best waffles in town." She stared at her wedding dress. "Looks like you need a fortifying meal."

Tilden shook his head. "She's not looking for crispy bacon. She wants a husband."

Maisey almost dropped her pot of coffee. "I've never put that one on the menu. You think it would be a good seller?" She filled Goldie's mug and walked away.

"I'm not your man. I'd rather poke myself in the eye with a dirty stick than get married." He took a ten from his wallet and set it on the table. "Coffee is on me."

He made to stand, but she gripped his hand and held it.

"Have you ever been so desperate that you'd do just about anything to get what you needed? I'm not talking about want here. I'm talking about a need as deep as hunger. In my case, it feels like starvation and homelessness. Ever been so alone that you had to rely on the kindness of strangers because you had no one else to depend on?"

His silent yes reverberated inside him. He'd been there. He was still there.

He sat down and leaned back in his chair. "What's your story?"

"You got an hour?"

"Yeah, I'm sure I do, but it looks to me like you have a deadline."

She picked up a napkin and tucked it into the bodice of her gown. "Can't afford to stain it. I have to ship it back to the designer tomorrow. Definitely can't afford to buy it."

His eyes grew wide. "You rented your wedding gown?"

She rolled her eyes. "No, I borrowed it. I'd never spend a dime on anything so ridiculous." She pointed to one crystal. "This little sparkly bit would pay for your breakfast."

He laughed. "You call it ridiculous, but you'll get married in it."

She let out a squeak. He was certain it was supposed to be a growl, but it caught in her throat and the pitch veered north.

"It's not a real marriage. Just a marriage of convenience."

He picked up his coffee and sipped while he looked over the rim. He was good at reading people, but he couldn't get a feel for this one.

"Not convenient for the groom or he'd be here. Seems rather troublesome to you at this point too."

She appeared to wilt. Her body sagged into the pouf of the dress. "My life is an inconvenience, but we're dealt the hand we're dealt, and we have to live with it."

"Or you can change it. What part of your life requires you to marry a stranger in a dress you wouldn't wish on your best friend?"

Her cheeks blushed. "Oh, I'd wish this and a case of pox on Stephanie, who used to be my best friend."

"Steal your groom?"

"No." She shook her head until her tiara nearly slipped off. "She stole my Hippy Chic sponsorship."

"You're speaking a foreign language."

Her phone rang and she groaned, holding up a finger when she answered. "Yes, I know I'm late. I'll be there in a few minutes." She hung up and looked at him like a seal before the slaughter.

He didn't know this woman, but he knew desperation when he saw it.

"I'm a social influencer who's lost her ability to influence." She pointed to her gown. "This was my last-ditch attempt to keep me out of the soup kitchen. I pimp products like this dress." She pointed to her lips. "Or this God-awful dried-blood red lipstick. I tell people how fabulously emollient it is and how the color is perfect for a night out. It feels like I've walked through an arid desert and my lips split." Her tongue slipped out to wet them.

"You lie to make money."

She laughed. "We all lie. Show me someone you consider honest, and I'll show you a fraud. Life isn't about the people, it's about the package."

There was some truth to her statement. Not everyone was forthright and honest, but she was wrong. Life was about the people.

"It's different if you lie to yourself as opposed to lying to others."

She shrugged. "Are you willing to help me lie? I need a temporary groom. We can get the marriage annulled next week for all I care."

She glanced down at the bills on the table.

"I'm not your man." He pointed between them. "Who would believe you'd marry someone like me?"

"Who would believe I'd have to marry someone at all? This wasn't part of my long-range plan, but sadly there isn't enough filler or Botox to keep me in business. At twenty-six I'm all washed up."

He lifted a brow. She was beautiful in that Hollywood airbrushed way, but no way was she twenty-six. "Another lie?"

She smiled a warm and genuine smile. "That's a secret."

"There's a difference?"

"Of course. A secret is an untold truth. A lie is pure fabrication. There is a difference, a secret cannot be a lie because it's kept."

"But you just told me you're twenty-six, which I believe is a lie."

"You would be correct, but my true age is a secret."

"You make my head spin."

"What do you say, can we get hitched?"

"Sorry, darlin', I'm not the marrying type. Isn't there another solution? No one would know if you were married or not."

"It's about the photos." She popped up. "What about this? You take a few photos with me and we'll call it a day."

He cocked his head. "That's still a lie."

"Not if we say nothing. What if I keep your face out of the photo?" She moved to the right to see his pants. "Perfect. You're wearing black."

"Thought this was a wedding, not a funeral."

"Depends on how you answer." She slid the five one-hundred-dollar bills across the table. "They're yours if you agree to take a couple of pictures with me."

"You'll pay me five hundred dollars to take a

picture?" He could use the money. He had at least a dozen soil samples that needed testing.

"Five hundred to take three pictures."

He plucked two of the bills from the pile. "I'll take two hundred for one."

He could see her thinking about his offer. It wasn't what she wanted, but what she'd get.

"Deal." She hopped up from her chair, grabbed the remaining three bills from the table and headed for the door. "You coming, honey?"

She breezed outside.

Tilden followed her.

All eyes were on him as he disappeared through the diner's glass door.

Goldie was already speaking to the limo driver, who was pulling off his jacket shirt and tie. She shoved a hundred into his pants pocket, then handed his clothes over.

"You want me to change into these?"

"I can't very well fake marry a man in a red flannel. It clashes with my lipstick." She climbed into the car and patted the seat next to her. "Come on in. I'll help you get ready."

He did as she asked, and the limousine started down the road. He didn't know why he wanted to help her, but he did. It could have been because all his life, he'd had to pretend to be someone he wasn't.

She went to work unbuttoning his shirt as if they'd been together forever. Her hands pushed the material back and off his shoulders. Her eyes grew big.

"Wow, you're well put together."

"I work outdoors."

"It suits you, along with that deep voice." She shook her head and went about getting him dressed again. Thankfully, the driver was on the plumper side.

When she had Tilden buttoned up and ready to go, she smiled. "You dress up well, too. Who would have thought?"

"Shouldn't judge a book by its cover."

Her nose scrunched. "Books ... why bother when you can watch the movie?"

He laughed. "I've got nothing to say to that."

She tugged at his tie and looked into his eyes. "I've got something to say." She placed her lips against his cheek. "Thank you for saving me today."

He straightened her crooked tiara and tugged the napkin she'd tucked into the neckline of her dress.

"You'll land on your feet." He believed she would. Goldie Sutherland wasn't who she appeared to be. He knew she was more, but was more always better?

"I hope so, but when I land, I pray it's in more comfortable shoes."

She knocked on the window and the driver opened the door.

"Let's do this."

Hand in hand, she walked him to where a photographer and a man in black waited by the tree.

She pulled the person in charge of the nuptials aside and whispered something to him before she pressed a bill into his palm.

She flagged Tilden over.

"Can we get one shot with the minister?" She looked toward the photographer. "He's camera shy, please don't get a direct shot of his face."

They were turned away when the click of the shutter filled the air. She squeezed his hand. "Sorry, I didn't know she'd take those."

"Let's give her a good shot. How about a kiss? One your people will talk about for days."

When she turned to face him, he cupped her cheeks and went for it. His lips pressed against hers. He didn't expect her to return the kiss, but when her lips parted and her tongue darted out to taste him, he didn't hold back. His hands wrapped around her waist, pulling her to him to deepen it.

She'd paid him two hundred dollars, and he wanted to make sure he delivered her money's worth. When he pulled back, she stared up at him. The kiss glistened on her lips.

"You kissed me."

He nodded. "I did and no lying, you enjoyed it."

She covered her kiss-swollen lips. "A girl never tells."

He winked at her. "We'll keep that our secret." He turned to the photographer. "Did you get that shot?"

She fanned her face. "Boy, did I get it."

Tilden had wood deliveries for the afternoon. Winter was here and people were still stocking up.

"I've got to go. You take care of yourself, okay?" He turned back to the limousine to get his clothes. The poor driver leaned against the rear quarter panel wearing black slacks and a white T-shirt. It was fairly warm for a January day, but the air was still brisk.

"Tilden," Goldie called. "You're the best."

He whipped around to face her. "That's a secret too. If you're ever in town again, look me up and tell me how it all panned out for you."

The feral man inside him wanted to race back and kiss her again. The methodical planner told him it was time to put his two hundred dollars to use. He almost felt guilty taking her money and the kiss.

She was in the wrong business. Her kisses were worth more than any affiliate income a tube of lipstick could provide. Goldie Sutherland had million-dollar lips.

CHAPTER THREE

Halfway through the drive back to Denver, Goldie's email lit up the screen. The photographer had sent her the one shot that would save her life along with the other fifty that would go a ways in filling her bank account.

Pictures of herself taken after Tilden left. Closeups of the lipstick, the tiara, the false lashes, the eyeshadow, the dress, and the heels. She was a walking billboard down to the nail polish and diamond on her ring finger.

She looked at the picture of the kiss. Wow, what a kiss. Who would have thought a bear of a man could pucker up like that? Funny thing was, she would have never given him a second glance on an average day and now she wondered if she'd be able to get him out of her mind.

His presence reinforced the idea that perception was based on the laws of supply and demand. Was the kiss twice as sweet because he'd been kind enough to help her for the paltry sum of two hundred dollars?

Her mind wandered again to the searing hot smooch. Had he taken it from her? He'd warned her. He started out slow and moved in for a deeper, more thorough kiss. Was that for her benefit or his? Was the laying on of lips his way of demanding a bonus for the job he didn't want but had completed?

Mr. Cool was a mystery. She smiled to herself and posted to her social media accounts.

Goldie got married.

She uploaded the picture that only showed the side of Tilden's face. His rugged beard was the focal point, at least to her. She'd never been a fan of facial hair. Now that she'd had that scruffy but soft feel against her cheeks, she could see the attraction. It felt better than the sandpaper-like material of the dress chafing her legs.

Her first response to the pic came in and gave her an idea. The follower asked who the man was. Goldie smiled. She simply put he was her little secret and after, she typed, #who'sTilden.

She kept her eyes on the screen, hoping to see her following skyrocket. Praying the ruse would pay off, but only a trickle of responses came in. Most weren't commenting on the products but her lack of transparency.

One person even had the audacity to accuse her of faking her marriage. Who would do that? It didn't matter that the insinuation was accurate, but why would the average person set up such an elaborate scheme? People were so untrusting these days.

She lowered the privacy screen to the driver.

"Ted, right?" she asked the man.

"Yes, ma'am."

"You saw my husband. Didn't it appear like a real wedding photo?"

He glanced at her from the rearview mirror. "I'm not an expert."

She raised her hand and pointed to her phone. "Neither is this person, but she's accusing me of setting up a shoot."

The poor man's brow shot so high, she thought it would leap off his face.

"Umm, it was a set-up, right? I mean, you basically kidnapped the man from the diner. You made him wear my clothes, and you took one real photo with him. I could see how some people might question that."

In her desperation, she never considered how fifty photos of the bride would look compared to one photo of the happy couple.

She pulled up the picture again and inspected it. It was hot. The way his hands cupped her cheeks. The thrust of his hips into the billowing tulle of her dress. The stretch of the almost too small jacket across his shoulders. How could anyone question the passion in that picture?

She zeroed in on his left hand. The one that faced the camera.

"Damn it."

"Are you okay, ma'am?"

"Holy mother of Mylanta."

"Ma'am?"

"Stop calling me ma'am. I'm Goldie." She tugged off the tiara and tossed it across the floor. The shoes went next. In a dramatic near swoon, she collapsed on the long black leather bench, a cloud of white fabric floating around her like a gaseous waste. "No ring."

"Excuse me?"

"He didn't have a ring."

"I'll leave you to your thoughts." The window went up.

When she tried to lower it again, it stayed put, as if the driver had child-locked her inside.

Sprawled on her back, she pulled her phone to her face and looked for additional tells.

Thankfully, Tilden wore black pants that were the exact color of the jacket, but when she got down to his shoes, she wanted to weep.

She had no idea what a person would call them. Hiking boots? Trailhead shoes? Big brown monstrosities with thick laces and hooks. The kind she imagined someone climbing Mount Everest would wear.

She was a person trained to watch the details, and she'd let two major things fall through the cracks.

Her groom was missing a ring, and he looked like he was ready to dash into the mountains to avoid her.

"Oh, holy hotcakes. This will never do."

She sent out an SOS to a few people she knew. Friends weren't something she had in this industry. It was a term used to describe someone being nice to you to get something they wanted.

The last time she had a bonafide friend was in high school and even then, as soon as "Growing Up Goldie" went off the air, her circle of friends dwindled. Everyone wanted their fifteen minutes of fame.

Elaine replied first.

Do you need a fire extinguisher?

That's exactly what she needed. Leave it to her number one rival to know.

No, just hoping you could share my wedding photo.

Goldie watched the three dots flash and scroll. Stall. Flash and scroll.

Sorry babe, that was news five minutes ago, but I love the Where's Waldo spinoff. You sure know how to hook them and reel them in. All two of them.

She knew she couldn't pull one over Elaine's eyes. She'd been in the business too long. She was the original Kardashian.

His name is Tilden.

Again, there were dots and stalls.

Who's Tilden?

Goldie sat up and laughed. That was the question. For all she knew, he was an indigent bootlegger.

That's the question everyone will be asking. Are you sure you don't want in on it?

A lifetime passed before she got an answer.

Fine. I posted, but you better be prepared to answer some questions

about the man. If this gets attention, inquiring minds will want to know.

Relief swept over her. She pulled up Elaine's site and scanned for the post, which was already buried by three after it. Elaine had cropped the photo, so it only showed their faces and his ring free hand. Who needed enemies when she had friends like Elaine?

Thanks.

She wanted to send her a more heartfelt emoji, but she figured a middle finger wouldn't be wise.

You owe me.

Goldie owed her all right. She owed her a size eight, bedazzled wedding shoe up the patootie.

If there was ever a time when she needed an intervention it was now. Desperation didn't look good on her, but at least the dress she'd been loaned did. She sent the pic off to her other "friends" and asked them to share. Most would treat her like she was asking them to infect a nation with cholera, but all she wanted was a little attention. Attention that would get people clicking.

How the mighty had fallen. Years ago, she had been a brand ambassador. People paid her to wear their clothes and makeup. Now she was relegated to affiliate ads and an occasional podcast.

She dialed her intended husband. Sebastian picked up on the third ring.

"I see you found a stand-in."

"A kiss in, anyway."

He let out a whistle. "I've never been so glad in my life not to marry you."

Her jaw dropped open. "What's that supposed to mean?"

"It means if I'd been the one in that kiss with you, Chloe would have castrated me. Who's the guy?"

She rolled her eyes. "It's Tilden and since you nearly ruined me today, you owe me. I need you to post something nice about us like you know us."

"It will be a lie."

She thought back to her and Tilden's conversation. "No, it's a secret."

"What do you want me to say?"

She considered it for a moment. "Something that makes it seem believable."

She could hear his fingers tapping on the keys.

"Done."

She pulled up his site.

A toast to Goldie and Tilden. He's

big and burly and she's, well … she's Goldie. Talk about opposites attract. Is this a reboot of the old "Green Acres" series? She's penthouse and he's pine trees. She's latte's and he's lager. She's a social icon and he's … #who'sTilden

"Thanks."

"What's next for you?"

She laughed. "A fake divorce, of course."

"He didn't actually marry you?"

"Why would he? He's obviously smarter than that."

She could almost see him shaking his head. It wouldn't take much time for some nosy person to put the pieces together, which meant she had to stay one step ahead of them.

"You may have saved my keister with that post. I may have to go with the opposites attract then attack. No one would believe I'd settle for mountain living when there's a new shopping center going up in Cherry Creek. You're a genius."

She pressed her blood red lips to the phone and gave him a virtual kiss.

"Good luck, Goldie."

Outside, the familiar scenery of her neighborhood passed by. The car stopped in front of the old miner's exchange. What had once housed millions of dollars in gold now housed her—or would as long as she could come up with the rent, which was a month past due.

"Got to go. There's a bottle of wine and a frozen dinner waiting for me inside." If she'd been talking to Elaine, she would have said a bottle of Cristal and Almas Russian Gold Caviar on toast points. Sebastian knew better. He'd seen her penthouse apartment. Elaine was still wondering.

Hank, the doorman, opened the glass doors of the building at the same time Ted opened the limousine door.

Goldie grabbed her shoes and her tiara, clutched them with her purse and phone to her chest, and made a mad dash to the door. It wasn't as if there would be a string of photographers in wait. That hadn't happened since her mom's funeral.

"Welcome home, Goldie," Hank said. "Where's the groom?"

She rushed into the elevator and laughed. "That seems to be the question of the day."

When the car stopped on her floor, she exited and walked into her home, dropping her wedding attire in piles as she went. To the average eye, it might appear that Tilden had stripped her on their way to the bedroom. She snapped a picture and posted, **Time for the honeymoon.**

In her lace panties and shelf bra, she opened the refrigerator. All that was left was the dregs of a box of white wine and a half-eaten box of Chinese takeout.

She carried them to the spot on the carpet where her sofa used to be and sat on the floor to stare at where her television used to hang on the wall. Oh, how the mighty had fallen.

CHAPTER FOUR

How many soil samples would he have to test before he could prove or disprove the rumors that his ancestors killed their rivals?

On the table in his cabin sat another dozen vials of dirt. Next to those was the diary of his great-great-grandmother, Treasure Coolidge. He opened it to the middle page. The part he'd read at least a hundred times. Old man Carver was dead. Cattle carcasses littered acres of land. The smell was so foul not even the vultures would fly overhead.

He'd followed the creek bed for miles. Sent sample after sample for testing, but all that came back were reports of nutrient-dense soil perfect for farming.

He'd come across his family mystery accidentally. He'd been told since he was knee-high that he was a Cool. The name Coolidge didn't enter his existence until his father died, and he inherited his father's belongings, which was comprised of a Colt 45 handgun and an old trunk with the hinges rusted shut.

Giving Tilden a trunk was like giving a robber the combination to the bank safe. All he had to do was get past the obstacles. He was a history buff and the old trunk intrigued him. It took him a full week to pry the lid open. He had no idea what he was looking at until he found a wedding dress wrapped in tissue paper and a diary. Everything inside belonged to Treasure. Her entire life had been shoved inside a wooden box.

He grabbed a soda from the refrigerator and made his way to his truck. Inside was his box. A box of empty vials he hoped one day would answer all the questions he had about his family.

He hated to enter the property during daylight. If what the diary suggested was true, then he'd be persona non grata.

He'd come to Aspen Cove two years ago when he found the name in Treasure's diary. There were several Aspen Coves around the country, but only one in the Rocky Mountains.

There was another clue when she mentioned Mount Meeker.

He popped the top of his soda and drank deeply. His life had been full of surprises since he'd arrived here. The latest being Goldie.

It had been several days since he'd kissed her and walked away. He wasn't sure why that kiss was still on his mind and his lips. Could be that she tasted like spun sugar, but more than likely it was because he hadn't kissed a woman in a long time. Years, actually.

Living off the grid in the mountains didn't lend itself to social calls. Few women would be thrilled with the amenities he offered. His shower was heated by the sun or firewood, and his water came from a pump in the back yard.

That was another surprise about Aspen Cove. He hadn't expected to like it here so much. Hadn't planned on staying, but when Ray Bradley offered him his couch, he couldn't refuse.

Then he got to know the local bootlegger Zachariah Tucker and he didn't have the heart to not help. The old duffer needed someone to deliver wood to his customers after one of his stills blew up and nearly burned off his arm.

He drove up the mountain road to the old

man's house, hoping he'd have a few deliveries. Maybe one to Abby Garrett.

Per usual, Zachariah was feeding the stills because once burned didn't make the old man twice shy. He'd upped his production because life was uncertain, and he didn't want to disappoint his best clients.

"Tilden, just the man I wanted to see." Zachariah walked over and spat a mouthful of sunflower seed shells that showered the forest floor in front of him.

"You got any deliveries?" With winter pressing forward, he was busier than usual, which was good. The money he'd make helped fill in where his editing job and research gigs fell short.

"I got a few." He pulled another handful of seeds from his pocket, stripping out bits of lint before he shoved them into his mouth. Once his cheek bulged, he continued. "Are you sure you won't deliver my mash?"

He made it sound like a takeout dinner, but it was the real thing. Mash was whatever Zachariah threw together to make his potent brew. Potato skins. Apple peels. Anything that could ferment and make alcohol.

"Not a drug runner. I told you before. I walk on the good side of the law."

"It's not illegal to homebrew."

They'd had this discussion many times. "Nope, but it's illegal to sell alcohol without a license."

The old man rubbed his beard, which had finally grown back after the last time he'd singed it to his chin from a fire that got away.

"It's not illegal to barter. I barter my brew for small pieces of green paper."

Tilden laughed. "Most people call that money."

Zachariah threw his arms in the air. "I call it happiness. Buys me a few dances at Buttercups. Got me a case of canned stew and some good videos from the pawnshop for when the next snowstorm hits."

There was no doubt in Tilden's mind the videos weren't action-adventure, unless "Debbie does Dallas" got reclassified.

"You're all set then. As for me, I'll take any firewood deliveries you've got, but I'm leaving the booze to you."

Zachariah kicked at the spent seeds on the ground. "How's that place of yours? Got water to the house yet?"

"I've got water, but not in the house."

He moved toward a trailer filled with two cords of firewood.

"If you upped your deliveries, you'd be able to run that last line to the taps. I know Ray was hoping to get it done before winter. Then the bastard had to die. But hell if he didn't do it in style. Fell straight into a set of double Ds and smothered to death."

Tilden tried not to laugh because dying wasn't a laughing matter, but everyone spun their own story about Ray's death, and he rather liked Zachariah's version even though the poor man had actually died from a heart attack.

"I think he was gone before he face-planted between Brandy's cleavage, but what a way to go. Whiskey in one hand and a stripper's ass in the other." He hoisted the trailer hitch and tugged the load the few feet to his truck before setting it in place. "Where's this delivery going?"

"One chord is going to the Dawsons', the other to Abby Garrett."

Tilden nearly jumped for joy. He knew Abby got her wood from old man Tucker and had been waiting to make a delivery. Ray had done it the last year so, outside of sneaking onto her property, Tilden had no reason to be there. But today changed that. The house sat at the far west of the acreage, which meant he'd have to travel the entire length of the land to get there.

"Did you already collect the money?"

"Yep, went straight to my PayPal account. I'll have your fees sent to yours before you bring the trailer back."

He gave Zachariah a playful punch to the shoulder. Handshakes were out of the question. Old man Tucker had running water, but Tilden wasn't sure if he ever used it. Grasping hands was like asking for a dose of the plague.

He climbed in his truck and headed straight for the Dawsons'. He wasn't responsible for stacking the wood. All he had to do was shove it off the tail of the trailer into a pile.

When he arrived, Basil was sitting on the porch. "Dad said you were coming."

Tilden walked around the trailer and unlatched the back. "Zachariah must have called to say I was on my way."

"I hate wood delivery day." He set a tray of brownies down and wiped his hands on his jeans. "I always end up with a splinter or two."

"Gloves, they're a wonder." He pulled a pair from his back pocket and tossed them to Basil. Poor kid had to live with that name, the least he could offer was a pair of gloves. He had three more pair in his glove compartment. "My gift to you if you share a brownie."

"Help yourself. They're day old but taste good just the same."

He climbed on the trailer while Basil put on the gloves. It only took a few minutes to shove the first load onto the ground.

"I hear you were swapping spit with some bride in the park. Good way to get your ass beat if you ask me."

Tilden laughed. "Didn't ask you. But she asked me."

"To stick your tongue down her throat? Where am I when something like that happens?"

"On the range or behind a range in the culinary school, I hear."

He tossed logs neatly into a stack by the front door. "No, seriously. Why is it that a girl comes into town, and I never know until the wedding is announced?"

"Whoa, wait a minute. I'm not getting married. She needed a groom. I sold her a few minutes of my time for two hundred dollars."

Basil stopped stacking wood. "Turning gigolo now?"

"Nope, she only wanted a picture. The kiss was a bonus."

"Aw, man, I would have kissed her for nothing. Word has it she was beautiful."

He hadn't considered her beauty all that much. She wasn't his type. Couldn't explain what compelled him to kiss her. It had simply happened.

"High maintenance. You know, the girl that spends her check and yours on boob jobs and facials."

"Never met one like that, but I'd like to."

He picked up a brownie from the pan and brought it to his nose. Day old or not, it smelled divine, just like Goldie. Only a brownie was a whole lot less trouble. A few bites and it would be gone for good. Then again, Goldie was gone as well.

"You need to broaden your horizons. Get down to the brewhouse. Venture into another town to meet some women your age."

"What's the opposite of a cougar?"

Tilden didn't know how to respond to that. "I have no idea. Why?"

Basil shrugged. "I have a thing for older women so what does that make me?"

"Like how old?" Was he talking grandma or a few years his senior?

"Just don't want to put up with the bullshit. I'm thinking anything between thirty and forty is good for me."

"How old are you?"

"I just turned twenty-four."

He rolled his eyes. "Stick with girls your age. The older ones will eat you alive."

Basil laughed. "That doesn't sound half bad either."

"You're still a puppy." He took a bite of the brownie and made his way to the driver's side of the truck. "I'm outta here."

"Thanks for chatting. I think that's the most I've heard you speak at one time."

He shrugged. "I'm more of a listener than a talker. Don't have much to say."

Basil lifted his chin. "See ya around."

Tilden climbed into his truck and headed toward Abby's. She was an odd one like him. She stuck to herself and didn't socialize. The only time he saw her out was when she had a crush on Thomas and was at the diner when he arrived. She did nothing but sit in a nearby booth and watch him.

In many ways they were alike. He wondered if she knew the history of her family, and if the long-ago scandal had molded her into the woman she was today. Every closet had a skeleton. Sometimes the bones hung there clanking noisily together. Sometimes they hid in a trunk, tucked in the center of an old pioneer's diary just waiting for discovery.

It took him nearly an hour to pass through

her property. Not because it was that long but because he stopped to take more samples from dry creek beds and areas where it was obvious water had run in the past. If his ancestors had poisoned the water, there would be traces of evidence left behind.

One reason he befriended Zachariah and Ray was because they were bootleggers and often their byproducts were dumped illegally. So far, nothing he'd tested from Zachariah's land proved poisonous.

There were definitely drunk animals from the hops and mash they consumed but nothing that would kill a herd of cattle or a man.

He passed a wall of white boxes, no doubt Abby's beehives, and hoped they were dormant. He didn't have a problem with the concept of raising bees, just an issue with their stings. Bees were territorial and he was trespassing.

Abby must have heard the trailer bouncing up the drive. The wood shifting and moving sounded like an avalanche or a rock slide. She popped out the front door and waved as he parked and exited the truck.

She was a pretty woman. Hard to tell how old she was, but he'd give her mid-thirties if the crinkling in the corner of her eyes was an accurate indicator.

"Tilden, it's good to see you." She held up a jar filled with amber. "I've got a few goodies for you. Honey. Soap. Lotion."

He walked toward her. "Thanks. I hear you make the best honey."

"I don't make it." She pointed in the distance to where the white boxes rose from the ground. "They make it, and I steal it from them."

"Where do you want the wood?"

"You going to stack it for me? That's not part of the deal, but I'll take it."

He looked at the bag in her hand. "Gifts aren't part of the package either, but I've got time, so why not?" He thought if he could get her talking about her land maybe he'd learn a thing or two. "If you help, we can get it done twice as fast."

"Deal." She handed him the bag and reached into her back pocket for a pair of gloves.

He dropped the bag into the cab and opened the bed of the trailer. It would have been easier to shove it off, but they picked it up by armfuls and carried it to the porch, where they stacked it near the front door.

"Has this property been in your family for a long time?"

She swiped a bead of sweat from her brow.

"Hundreds of years. It's Carver property.

My mom was a Carver, although she never held the name. Her mom was a Kirkenheifer and my dad was a Garrett. It's all so muddled after so many marriages."

"Did your family always raise bees?" He already knew the truth, but wondered if she did and if so, would she tell him?

"No, they raised cattle." She let out a visible shiver. "Thank goodness that's not the case these days. Besides their gaseous habits ruining the air, they eat everything in sight. What would my bees pollinate if the land was filled with cows?"

"Oh, so there were cattle? What stopped this from being a cattle ranch? Lack of water?" He lifted a brow. "On my way over I noticed most of the creeks are dry beds."

"You're observant." She tossed another log onto the pile and leaned against the deck railing. "Water doesn't run naturally on this land. The landscape is too high and therefore runs on the acreage next door. Thankfully the creek on the acreage next to mine is alive and healthy, because you can't have bees without water."

"Or flowers." He continued to stack the wood.

"You may be quiet, but you're smart."

"Not smart enough to figure out how a family raises cattle on dry land."

"Why the interest?"

He was winded from the constant unloading and stacking and leaned against the deck rail near her.

"I'm a history buff and love to dig into the story of places. Aspen Cove has quite a lot of history with its founding fathers."

When she frowned, he thought maybe he'd dug too deep.

"It's definitely got some stories." She moved to the door and opened it. "You want some sweet tea?"

If he could fist-bump the air without looking like a total idiot, he would have. "I'd love some."

"Come inside."

He followed her into the single-story log cabin. The main living area was wide open, with the kitchen, dining room and living room one big, happy space. In the center of one wall sat a huge moss rock fireplace that went from floor to ceiling.

"This is a great house."

When he'd first moved in with Ray, the walls were covered with animal trophies. He'd taken them down and built the bookcases. He'd trade a deer head for a collection of Hemingway any day.

She opened the cupboard and grabbed two

glasses. They were the kind that looked like jelly jars from the sixties. They were the same flowered glasses his grandmother once had.

"You bought Ray's place, right?"

"No, he left it to me. Crazy man, but he didn't have any family, and I love the place. It's private. I like my space."

"Me too." She grabbed a pitcher from the refrigerator and poured them both a glass.

He drank half his down and she filled it again.

"This is the same house that was here in eighteen forty-seven when Walton Carver homesteaded the place."

"Wow, lots of history then."

"You know history, there's some good and some bad." She sipped her tea and pulled out a chair at the table and pointed to the one next to her for him. "As for the cattle. It was a big operation. Supplied food to thousands until they all dropped dead."

His tea glass slipped from his hand, spilling over the table. "Sorry." He jumped up and grabbed the towel sitting on the counter to clean up his mess.

"No worries. It's just tea. It's not like you killed off my family's cattle."

He held his breath for a second. "What happened?"

"Tragic really. Some kind of water rights fight with a family called the Coolidges."

He stalled mid clean-up. "What do you know?"

She shrugged. "Not much. Only that they were tired of the cattle running across the land to get water. The cows ate up the wheat and hops they grew for their moonshine."

"I read something about that." He'd read in detail about all the hours it took for Treasure and her family to fence off the property, only to have sections downed the next week.

"What you probably didn't read about was how the Carvers diverted the water. It crossed their property in one spot, and they damned it off there. If you ask me, that's where all the problems began."

It fascinated Tilden because diverting the water wasn't listed in any of the historical documents he'd received. He could see the water paths had changed, but then they were restored not too far after, and he'd considered it a natural drought occurrence.

"They diverted the creek?"

"Oh, yes. Blocked the water from reentering

the Coolidge land. I hear it was a real mess. They tried to trench out a path, but the water had its own mind, which was to disappear and bubble up into a natural pond a few acres away. My family thought it was a godsend, but weeks later, the cattle died off and so did Walt. Rumors spread that the Coolidges poisoned the pond with their leftover rotted mash. Some even said they turned the pond into a pool of moonshine and the cattle and Walter died from alcohol poisoning."

He processed this information. He was certain his ancestors didn't waste enough moonshine to fill a pond, but he was interested in learning about where the water disappeared to.

"Where is the lake now?"

She shook her head. "No idea. The story was it dried up and the creek broke through its barriers to right the wrong."

"You think the Carvers were wrong?"

She rose from the table and put both of their glasses in the big farmers sink. "I think they could have come up with a solution that didn't require either to have exclusive access to the water. I can't say if they poisoned the pond, but karma is a bitch that won't go unanswered and diverting the water seemed to be the start of the problems."

They walked outside and went back to

stacking wood. "What happened to the Coolidges?"

"Not sure. The scuttlebutt is they were run out of town, but who knows? They could have been guilty and ran. We'll never know."

Tilden finished stacking the last log. He'd made a promise to himself two years ago that he would find out the truth.

"Who owns the property now?"

"That's a mystery too. Bea Bennett owned it. Always said the whole thing was a tragedy. She never did anything with the land. She died, but no one has come to claim it. Someone owns it, but the million-dollar question is who?"

"What if it's a cattle rancher?"

She laughed. "Well, wouldn't that be irony?" She walked him toward his truck. "I have to believe that even if it were a rancher, we could behave differently than our ancestors."

Tilden sighed. He knew he had no claim to the land. His family had been gone for over a hundred years and it had changed hands several times. There was no doubt in his mind someone would eventually claim it and he hoped for Abby's sake whoever did wouldn't start another feud over something silly.

CHAPTER FIVE

Goldie's messenger account lit up like a Christmas tree for days after the "wedding." They weren't the messages she'd hoped to see, but scathing ones about false advertising and milking the system for what it was worth. Of course, she'd milk the system. The system created her. She was born into it and imagined she'd die collecting from it, but she didn't expect that death to happen so soon.

Despite her friends posting about her wedding, her reach continued to decline, and her presence became more of a joke than anything else.

She thought about the many days her mother had locked herself inside her bedroom and cried.

Back then, Goldie thought she was insane to worry about what people thought of her. Now with a pile of bills as tall as the Eiffel Tower, she understood it wasn't about what people thought but how they responded.

Like her mother, if people didn't follow her career, they weren't financially invested. Back then, that meant Liza Sutherland couldn't pay her bills. Couldn't feed her kid. No wonder she was willing to go under the knife for a chance to share the screen with several other has-beens. Aging sucked, but who would have thought Goldie Sutherland would be washed up at thirty-two?

She tore open the dozen or so new bills sitting on her counter. She hated mail of any kind. It took her hours to work through them. Hated emails for the same reason. Hated the letters. Hated the fonts.

Past Due

Delinquent

Due Now

They all meant the same thing. Someone wanted money she didn't have.

When her stomach grumbled, she pushed off the kitchen counter to open the refrigerator. Inside was a bottle of ketchup and a loaf of bread.

How long could a person live off ketchup sandwiches?

She still had one hundred dollars left. She'd tucked it into her wallet for an emergency. Starving counted as dire need in her book.

She slid on her shoes and grabbed her purse. When she opened her apartment door, the yellow eviction notice floated down to land at her feet.

It was the second one she'd gotten in the last week. She picked it up and crumpled it in her fist before she tossed it into her apartment.

When the elevator arrived in the lobby, the doorman stood behind the desk eyeing her. He was newer and always seemed to wear a frown and have a chip on his shoulder.

He nodded. "Ms. Sutherland."

She looked at his name badge, which read Derek Manly. He was a tall, spindly young man whose stature didn't fit his name.

"Mr. Manly." A giggle bubbled up inside her that she forced back. It wouldn't serve her any good to piss off the doorman.

He lifted his phone and showed her what he'd been looking at. The leading gossip columnist headline read, "Goldie Sutherland turns from gold dust to dust."

"Don't believe everything you read. Gold

doesn't turn into dust." She gave him a practiced smile. "Gold turns into jewelry. I'm still as shiny and valuable as always." She headed for the door.

He chuckled. "If you value antiques."

She stopped dead. "I'm sorry, do you like your job here? The last time I looked, your job was supposed to be helpful to the residents."

He rolled his slate gray eyes. "Paying residents."

It took everything inside her not to swing her five-year-old Prada bag at his head. Housing would be a problem for her soon, but she wasn't ready to trade her current situation for a jail cell.

"I'm a little behind is all."

"You can lie to yourself, but you can't lie to me. Your landlord called and said if I saw you to tell you to have your past due rent by the end of the week or he'd help move you out himself."

She stood tall. "If you talk to Mr. Page, tell him I said everything is under control." She pushed through the glass door into the wintery chill of the afternoon.

Tugging her jacket up to her chin, she walked down the street to the little store that carried everything from Cracker Jacks to Parma ham. She was relieved to see the Christmas decorations were already down. This year she'd spent the holiday eating a plate of cookies a neighbor made and streaming Netflix. There was no tree. No decorations. No gifts.

"Hello, Goldie," Cindy said from behind the counter. She'd taken over for her grandmother about a year ago when Mrs. Hutchins had a stroke.

"How's your grandmother?" She'd always loved the little old lady. Trudy Hutchins was like a grandmother to all.

"She's doing so well." Cindy moved from around the counter to where Goldie stood. She pulled out her phone and brought up the latest pictures of Trudy. "We gave her a surprise birthday party last week." Her eyes grew wide. "She's eighty."

After pulling five packages of Ramen from the counter, Goldie said, "I feel like I'm eighty."

Cindy put her hand on Goldie's shoulder and gave her a squeeze. "Things will get better."

"They will have to because worse isn't on my agenda."

"Grams always says God puts you where he wants you."

God must want me to live in a box behind the store.

"Tell your Grams I said hello." She set her purse on the counter and dug for the hundred-dollar bill she'd tucked inside the zipper pocket.

"She loves to hear that." She rung up the packages of ramen. "That will be three dollars and forty-eight cents." After placing them into a bag she asked, "Are you sure you don't want a package of chicken or some fresh veggies to go with that?"

Cindy was probably in her mid-twenties. There was no doubt in Goldie's mind that she made more money pimping groceries in her grandmother's store than Goldie did pushing products like lipstick and wrinkle cream.

"Things are bit tight right now, this money is going to have to last me for a while. I'll stick with what I have." She handed over the last of her money and waited for her change.

Cindy held up her finger. "Hold on a second." She raced around the counter toward the back room and returned with a filled bag. "Take this. It's not much, but it's still good. I'd normally donate it to the homeless shelter, but charity begins at home. The expiration dates are today, but if you freeze it, you can get more time from the products." She opened the bag to show several packages of meat and a couple of frozen dinners.

Tears pricked at Goldie's eyes. Was she crying because she was touched or because her life had come to this? When would she have to stand on the corner with a cardboard sign that said, "anything helps"?

"Thank you. That's so kind."

Cindy made change for the ramen. "It's nothing." She looked down at Goldie's bag. "I love that purse. They don't make it anymore."

Goldie ran her hand over the soft calf's leather. This had been a prized possession for years. "No, they retire products early."

"If things are terrible, you could sell it. Those things never go down in value and never go out of style."

Goldie smiled. Behind the ponytail and the sprinkling of freckles that dotted Cindy's skin was a diva waiting to break free.

"Do you have an extra bag?"

"Sure." Cindy reached beneath the counter and pulled a white plastic bag free.

It only took Goldie a few moments to empty the purse of all her belongings. She took it over to the nearby trashcan and turned it upside down, shaking the bits of lint and garbage into the bin. When she returned, she zipped it up and set it on the counter like it was on display.

"For you."

Cindy's mouth dropped open. "I can't take your purse. Why would you give this to me?"

Goldie smiled as she picked up her plastic bags. "Because kindness has value and never goes out of style." She turned and walked outside.

Her life was a mess, but it was in small moments like this where she found the will to forge on.

The brisk wind beat against her face until she made it back to her building. She pushed inside and stopped when she saw her landlord in the lobby talking to Derek.

This would be the best time to not draw attention to herself. If she could sneak past them and scurry into the elevator, she'd be home free.

Skirting the outside of the room, she drifted toward the corner. She pretended she didn't see them and hoped somehow that would make them not see her. She reached for the up button and breathed a sigh of relief before she heard her name.

Pretending to be hearing impaired, she ignored her landlord calling after her and hoped the doors would open and suck her inside.

A glance at the display showed the car was on the third floor. "Come on," she whispered. "Come on." Her booted foot tapped on the granite floor.

A shadow took up whatever light the windows cast on her.

"Do you have the rent?"

She turned to face Mr. Page. "Good afternoon, Mr. Page. I was going to call you."

"No need. I'm here. Do you have the rent?"

She lifted her head to take in the big man. Always dressed in custom suits, he was quite the figure. She might call him handsome if she liked well-dressed ogres, but Mr. Page's godfather persona was a turnoff. If John Gotti and Shrek had a baby it would look like the man in front of her.

"I do not, but I will."

"You have until Friday. If I don't have it by then I'm changing the locks."

She pulled back her shoulders. "I understand."

The elevator opened and she rushed inside. When the doors closed, her calm façade fell to pieces. She had two days to come up with thousands of dollars.

"Desperate times require desperate measures." She punched the P for the penthouse. When she arrived back at her home, she tucked her groceries away and walked to her closet. She'd already sold everything else in the house. Even her mattress sat on the floor because the sale of the frame helped make her last car payment. And by last car payment, she meant final. The damn thing was the only thing she owned outright.

She'd debated selling it, but a used car wouldn't get her much and if everything went farther south at least she could sleep in the back seat.

She threw open her closet. On shelves that lined one wall sat her equivalent of the Oscar. Limited edition accessories and clothes. Cindy was right about one thing. Couture items rarely lost their value.

It was hard to say goodbye to so many beautiful things, but she needed money more than she did shoes and purses, so she selected one purse to keep and a few pairs of shoes, and the rest she listed online for sale.

Donated food and a fire sale of her belongings. What had her life become?

CHAPTER SIX

Tilden sat at the end of the bar oblivious to the comings and goings at Bishop's Brewhouse. The din of the crowd acted as the backdrop to his thoughts. He'd spent the day in Copper Creek where they housed all the historical documents. Poring through dozens of files, he couldn't find the smoking gun or the answers to his questions, but he met a nice records keeper who said she'd pull the older land maps.

"What'll it be, Tilden?" Sage leaned forward to get his attention.

"Amber draft, please."

She moved to the taps and pulled him a beer. "You need a job?"

"What?" he yelled over the cacophony of the crowd and karaoke night singers. Each time Samantha came to the bar, the crowds grew. There was enough room to stand and turn but not much more. He lucked into the corner stool because from this seat there was nothing to see.

"I may need to hire someone soon." She pointed to Cannon, who was pouring a round of shots. "We can hardly keep up on Thursday nights. Forget about Friday and Saturday."

He looked around. "Good for business though."

It was almost eight o'clock, which meant the singers would lay down their mics and head home to put their kids to bed. Small towns were like that. The sidewalks rolled up after dark.

Tilden picked up his beer and swiveled his stool to face the small stage.

He'd been in Aspen Cove going on two years. When he arrived, the Brewhouse was the only thing that stayed open most of the week. The diner used to have winter hours on Tuesday, Thursday, and Sunday, but now was open seven days a week. The bar was closed on Sunday. The corner store was hit and miss. The dry goods store was closed now because people were too busy to sell their crafts and homemade goodies.

He'd gotten his favorite knit hat there. The townsfolk teased him because Mrs. Brown had made it. They said it wasn't yarn at all but hair from her cat Tom. He didn't care where the material came from, it was the softest hat he'd ever owned.

"What have you been up to?"

"Not too much."

He sipped his beer and swung around to face her. Behind her back, everyone called Sage the little leprechaun, but to her face, they called her ma'am because she demanded respect, plus she basically ran the clinic, and she'd suggested things like tetanus shots and rectal exams for those who irritated her. He always tried to stay on her good side.

"Hear you got married."

He almost choked on his beer. "No, ma'am. I was faking it for a friend." He had no idea why he called Goldie a friend. He didn't know her, but he'd kissed her, and that kind of made him more than an acquaintance.

"Did you know you're all over the internet?"

"I'm what?" He pulled his phone out and searched for Goldie. When her full name came up, he clicked on the first site. It was some kind of blog she ran.

Sage's fingers rushed over the screen of her phone and held it up to show him the one picture he'd allowed. He couldn't see his face, but his first name was posted in all the comments. Who's Tilden? Where's Tilden? We need more Tilden. #Tilden.

Sage pulled back her phone and looked at the screen. "She's telling everyone her husband is shy and a bit reclusive but a damn sexy mountain man."

He laughed. "That wasn't a lie." He found it funny that she'd pegged him accurately in the few minutes they spoke. He was quiet and a loner. He couldn't speak to the sexy part. He wasn't his type.

Sage snapped a picture of him. "You're like a new game." She typed something and then posted his picture. When she turned the screen around, she'd caught him mid-sip and all she wrote was, #Tilden.

"What's the story there?"

He shrugged. "Can't say. She needed a groom, and all I was willing to offer was a picture."

"Do you know who she is?" She didn't wait for him to answer. "She used to be a big social media influencer. If she wore it, everyone bought it. Her mom was a starlet in her day but died a few years ago."

"That's a shame."

"What about you? You got parents?"

He rested his back against the wall. He wasn't a chatty guy so all this *kumbaya let's get to know you* was out of his comfort zone.

"Everyone has parents. Mine are dead too." She didn't need to know his mother died from an aneurysm when he was fifteen, no doubt from screaming at his drunk father, who'd died from pancreatic cancer several years ago.

"Mine too."

He felt bad for being short. "Sorry to hear that."

"What is it you do? I always thought you were a bootlegger."

He laughed because that seemed to be the consensus. He rarely corrected anyone because a reputation as a bootlegger made people steer clear.

"Nope. I leave the moonshine to Zachariah. As for me ... I dabble in a lot of stuff. All legal." Did he dare tell her he had a degree in history and had once taught high school American Government classes? Was it important for her to know he'd written several books on small towns like Aspen Cove? That he edited manuscripts and researched topics for money? Probably not. "I have a love for everything books."

She picked up the bar towel and wiped off the condensation that dripped on the counter from his beer.

"You know what I've always wanted for this town?"

He lifted a brow. "You mean for the two plus years you've been here?"

She flung out the towel like a whip and caught him up the side of his head. "Smartass."

He nodded. "You got the smart part right."

"Seriously, wouldn't it be great if the old Dry Goods Store was turned into a bookstore that sold real coffee? Not pod brewed but espressos and lattes?"

There was some merit to that. If they had a bookstore in town, he'd save on gas going to Copper Creek.

"A bookstore sounds nice."

Her green eyes lit up. "There could be a kid's section with story hour. At night, what about an adult hour where scary or sexy books were read? How does a book club sound?"

"What's got you all worked up, baby?" Cannon wrapped his arms around Sage's waist and kissed her cheek.

"Your wife wants you to buy the vacant store and open her a book shop."

She grabbed his half-empty beer and topped it off. He never had to pay for more than one, and it never seemed to empty.

"No. I want Tilden to buy the shop and open a book store. He says he loves books."

Cannon lifted both brows carving a wrinkle in his forehead. "Books you say?" He shrugged. "Learn something new every day. So, are you going to do it?"

"Do what?" came a familiar voice from his right.

"Tilden here is going to open a book store." Cannon placed a napkin and pen in front of Doc, who took the now empty stool next to Tilden.

This was their thing. Each night, Doc came for a beer and a game of Tic Tac Toe. He only had to pay for his beer if he lost. Doc rarely lost. Or maybe Cannon always let him win.

Doc lifted the mug to his lips and took a long draw. The suds stuck to his mustache until his tongue darted out to swipe the foam away.

"Is that so?" He picked up the pen and drew a nine-box grid before marking the center with an X.

"No, it's not so. I need plumbing that comes

all the way to my house before I can buy a book store."

Doc rubbed his beard while Cannon filled in the upper right with an O. They went back and forth until the game was over, and Doc was drinking free.

"It's not a terrible idea." Doc drew squiggles in the frost of his mug.

Tilden shook his head. "While I have a passion for books, I hate showering outside in the winter."

Sage gasped. "You shower outside? What do you do? Rub an ice cube over your body?"

She was close to being right.

"No, I have an old still I put on stilts. I light it up about an hour before I want to shower. If it's bitter cold outside I need two hours to heat it. Gravity pulls the water down the hose."

She turned to Cannon. "Next time I complain about anything, remind me that Tilden showers outside."

"You all heard it." Cannon moved to the register to cash out the last of the wannabe singers.

"Time to stock." Sage disappeared into the back room.

"You and I have had little time to get to know one another," Doc said. "Tell me about yourself."

He wanted to groan, but that would have

been disrespectful. "I'm a history buff. I've heard you come from a family that built Aspen Cove." He hoped that Doc was like most people. Once they got to talking about themselves, they forgot they'd asked any questions.

"Yes, I am. I hear you're living in Ray Bradley's old place."

"Yep, he left it to me in his will."

"You kin?"

Tilden shook his head. "Nope, just helped him out at the end and he was kind to me."

"Ray's family is an interesting story if you like gossip." He lifted his bushy brows as if it was a question.

"Really? What makes his story worthy?" Ray seemed like simple folk. He didn't ask for much. He didn't get much. He once told Tilden that he could have everything he wanted if he wanted nothing. What was the fun in that?

"Tell me."

"Can't confirm it, but rumor had it the Bradleys came about when Walt Carver had an affair with Virginia Coolidge. She was married to Eton Bradley at the time." Doc looked at Tilden. "I always thought you were related to Ben."

"No, sir." That was an instinctual answer, but he probably was related. He'd never heard of

Virginia Coolidge, but then again, maybe she was the Ginny who Trudy mentioned in her diary. He stored that information away for future reference.

"My family wagon-trained it over from the east. They hired a Major Phelps to guide them to the Rockies. Truth was they were headed for California and the gold they'd been hearing about, but they got here and stayed."

"Fascinating. Were there other families with them?" He knew there were but found it better to not lead people. The information was pure when it wasn't pulled from someone.

"Sure. The Carvers were always in that group headed for California and the Coolidges, and the Bennetts. I'm sure you've heard of Bea. She's like the Mother Teresa of Aspen Cove."

He nodded. "I hear she was a mighty fine woman."

Doc sipped his beer. His bright eyes seemed to dim. "We lost a good one."

"If they were determined on getting rich mining for gold, what did they do here to make a living?"

"Cattle. My ancestors were ranchers as were the Carvers and the Bennetts. Although Walt Carver did his best to find gold on his land."

That spiked Tilden's curiosity. "He mined for gold?"

"That's what I heard. Dug a tunnel halfway across his land. Damn fool thought he'd strike it rich. Instead, he ended up dead."

Tilden's heart beat so hard he could barely breathe. "Any idea how he died?"

"He spent most of his days in those tunnels. Gasses build up. Poor oxygen quality. They didn't have forensics back then, so we'll never know."

"You're a fountain of knowledge."

"I hear you got married. Where's the bride?"

Tilden let out a sigh. "She already left me. Found out I lived in the woods and raced to the limousine before we could sign the papers."

Doc looked at him sternly. "Are you yanking my chain, son?"

Tilden nodded. "Yes, sir, I am. I didn't get married. Merely got paid to pose for a picture."

Doc emptied his beer. "She was quite a looker. Pretty thing in that cloud of white."

Tilden remembered Doc being in the corner hiding behind his paper. "So you saw her. She may be pretty, but a woman like Goldie Sutherland is nothing but trouble."

Doc patted Tilden's back. "Son, all women

are trouble." He slid off his stool. "Speaking of trouble, I need to get back to my Agatha."

Doc laid a five on the bar and left.

Tilden flagged Cannon over to pay for his beer. When his tab was clear, he walked outside with less money in his pocket but a whole lot more information moving through his brain.

CHAPTER SEVEN

Goldie pocketed the hundred-dollar bill and smiled at the new owner of her favorite Chanel bag.

"I can't believe I got this for a hundred bucks." The twenty-something with perky boobs and an early addiction to fillers bounced on her heels and nothing moved but the flounce of her Dior dress.

"It's a great deal." Given the purse was well over a thousand dollars new and had been used only a handful of times, it was downright robbery.

"Did you say you were moving?"

Goldie looked around her empty apartment.

Moving was the best story she could come up with.

"Yes." She licked her pomegranate lips. "You may have seen it on my blog ... I got married."

The girl moved to the window. The penthouse sat at the top floor of the Miner's Exchange building and overlooked the city of Denver.

"Great view. Have they rented the place yet?"

"What's your name?" Goldie would have guessed Solange or Monique or something like that.

"Courtney."

Wouldn't have picked that one for the bottle blonde with a thousand lowlights. "I believe they already rented it out." She didn't want Courtney putting out feelers. Any interested party with a pulse and a paycheck would have her landlord's ear.

Her lower lip stuck out. "Tell me about Tilden."

Goldie wanted to fist pump the air. If she knew his name, then she'd been paying attention. "Oh, he's..." She took in an exaggerated breath that lifted her chest before she exhaled into a sigh. "He's amazing."

Courtney reached for her left hand and

stared at the empty ring finger. It was an oversight for sure. The entire wedding outfit had had to be returned, including the jewelry she'd borrowed from Carbon.

"No ring? Don't tell me your mountain man is a cheapskate."

"No." She giggled to hide her lie. "It's being resized."

Courtney walked away from the window toward the door with her new bag tucked under her arm. "You are fluffier than I expected." She looked Goldie up and down. "And a lot older."

She opened the door and hoped the woman left quickly because if she didn't, she was likely to get beaten with the bag she'd purchased.

"Thanks for coming by. I've got to go." She tapped the cell phone she had in her hand. "Lunch with Tilden."

"Oh, where are you meeting? I'd love to see him."

Goldie started to close the door and just before the lock clicked, she said, "In bed. He has a serious appetite. No time for visitors."

The last she heard from Courtney was, "Oh my."

Back in her room, she rummaged through what was left. She'd sold most of her bags, a few pairs of her shoes and several couture dresses.

Clothes were hard because most of the items with value were custom designed for her body. In her heyday, she'd been likened to Marilyn Monroe with a 36-24-36 figure. The reality was more like 36-28-40 these days.

She thought about Courtney's comment about her weight and age. Obviously, she couldn't get away with telling people she was twenty-six. There wasn't enough Botox to freeze her laugh lines.

Emptying her pockets, she counted out the bills. Why she'd moved into a place with rent that breezed past three thousand a month was beyond her. No doubt it was because back then, everyone was watching. Everyone was buying.

People thought she made a fortune and she did, but it cost a fortune to keep up the lifestyle they tuned in to see. A vicious damn circle of earn and spend.

Eighteen hundred dollars sat in a pile at the end of her bed and she was still thousands short.

She flopped onto the comforter and looked at her phone. She'd been watching the numbers daily. Her affiliate accounts were trickling in with income, but it was barely enough to buy new underwear. It wouldn't pay her rent. The largest earnings came from the lipstick which in her opinion looked like blood from a day-old crime scene.

A ping sounded, which meant her blog had an active visitor. When she clicked on the comments, she wanted to scream. Little Courtney had been busy. Goldie read every painful word in slow motion.

Goldie isn't so golden anymore. Social icon is old and fluffy, and all washed up. #whereisTilden

"It's who's Tilden, you twit." She buried her head in her pillow and screamed. She lay there for an hour lamenting about her life and the turn it had taken.

Her publicist's ringtone pulled her from the abyss. Nancy always had good news and if she didn't, she always had a plan.

"Nancy, I'm so glad to hear from you. What have you got for me?"

"Hey, Goldie. You got a minute?"

She rose from the mattress and walked through the hall to the kitchen. Even her bare feet echoed through the space.

"Sure. Please tell me you've got good news for me. Things have been slow here lately."

The silence that met her was sharp and cold, like a steel blade to her gut.

"This isn't that kind of call. Your kind of career is like produce at the grocery store. It's great while it sits on the shelf and looks pretty, but even an apple has an expiration date."

"You're comparing me to an apple?"

"Oh, Goldie. I'd say you were a peach, but they spoil faster. Your time in the spotlight is up."

The lump in her throat burned like a ball of fire. "Are you quitting me?"

"I don't like to say the word quit, but I can't promote something no one wants."

She fell against the cabinet and slid to the floor. Without Nancy, she had less than the nothing she had now because without her publicist there were no deals to be brokered. No Fendi. No Marc Jacobs. No Chanel. No Lancer. No Maybelline. Nothing.

There weren't any words left to be said. Nancy had said them all: no one wanted her. "Okay, Nancy. Thanks for everything."

This was it. She'd give her landlord what she could gather and hope he'd let her stay until she found a better situation. She thought about the friends she could call for help. There was no one, because in her business friends and enemies were only separated by a deal or a paycheck. It was a dog eat dog world, and she'd just been devoured.

She found the strength to rise and made her way to her bedroom, where she scooped the money off the bed. In the morning, she'd head to the bank and get a cashier's check for Mr. Page. Surely, he'd be sympathetic to her plight.

GOLDIE WOKE AND THEN SHOWERED. She pulled herself together even though she was falling apart. In her head, her mother's three rules played repeatedly.

It isn't over until it's over.

There's always time for another curtain call.

Look like a star even though you feel like a meteor.

She tucked the eighteen hundred-dollar bills into her purse. Fifteen hundred would go to Mr. Page to show good faith that she was trying. Three hundred would stay in her wallet so she could eat and put gas in her car.

Once she was put together, she glanced in the mirror. "You may be nothing and have less, but no one else knows. Fake it until you make it." She leaned in and stared at the lines branching out from the corners of her eyes. Mom always told her she'd regret those days in the sun and boy did she.

She pulled out her black sharpie and touched up the heels of her boots before she grabbed her coat and walked out. The elevator arrived to take her down and when she exited, a smiling Derek greeted her.

"Good morning, Ms. Sutherland."

"Good morning, Derek. You're in good spirits."

"I'm earning a bonus today." He walked to the door and held it open. "Will you be gone long?"

She rather liked the smiling Derek.

"Running to the bank and then to grab a bite to eat." She was really stopping by the corner coffee shop for a muffin and a tea, but he didn't need to know. "Can I bring you anything?"

"I'd love a latte if you're passing a coffee shop."

She frowned on the inside but smiled on the surface. A damn latte would put her back at least three bucks, but she supposed a rare smile from Mr. Manly was worth it.

"Sure thing. I'll see you in about an hour."

"Take your time."

One step outside reminded her that her life wasn't so warm and fuzzy. The chill of the morning air sank into her bones. She trudged up the street toward an uncertain future.

It took a half an hour to run her errands. She sat in the coffee shop eating her muffin and sipping her English breakfast tea.

The sign on the door said they were hiring. Goldie chewed her lip trying to get the courage to ask for an application. No job was beneath her, but she'd fallen so far. She likened it in her mind to going from the President of the United States to being the president of the PTA.

Never in her life had she applied for a job before. However, starvation and homelessness looked less appealing than asking for an application. Before she could lose her nerve, she got up and walked to the register.

"Can I help you?" asked the girl who had made her tea.

"I see you're hiring?"

The cashier nodded. "You got a kid looking for a job?"

Goldie's head snapped back. There was no way she looked old enough to have a working-age child. That would mean she would have given birth at sixteen or younger. It was a possible scenario, but geez, did the world have to kick her with steel-toed boots while she was down?

"No, it's for me."

The girl's head sprang back. "Oh, right." She reached under the counter and pulled out a packet of papers. No less than five sheets were attached. "Fill these out and bring them back. The owner is interviewing for the position next week."

She picked up the stack of papers. "Is there a shorter application? You don't need a security clearance to sell coffee, do you?"

"Nope, but that's the one they use here."

Goldie took it back to the table. "I feel like an organ donor," she said louder than she wanted.

"Oh, that's for certain. Working here will suck your soul straight from your body."

"Great." She sipped her tea and stared at the first page. It would take her several days to get through the application. She didn't have that kind of time today, so she folded the pages in half and put them in her purse. She was on her way out the door when she remembered Derek's coffee.

A pivot on her boots brought her back to the counter to order his latte. Three dollars and fifty-nine cents later she was headed back to her building with his drink in one hand and a cashier's check in her purse. Things weren't looking up, but she hadn't hit rock bottom. She still had her pride and two packages of ramen.

Derek was behind the counter when she arrived. She slid his latte across the smooth marble finish.

"Here you go."

"Thanks, Goldie."

It was odd he used her first name, as they were required to address the residents formally. Movement to her right drew her attention. Mr. Page followed a man pushing a hand cart full of boxes.

"Oh, Mr. Page." She hurried toward him, the heels of her boots thwacking against the granite floor. "I've got money for you." She opened her purse and pulled out the check. "It's not everything, but it's something."

He adjusted his tie and reached into his jacket pocket for a pair of glasses he then balanced on the bridge of his nose.

"This is a bonus." He smiled at her and held out his hand. "I'll need your keys."

Heart was all she had left but hers did a high dive and landed in the pit of her stomach. "Why? I just gave you money."

"For last month, Goldie. This month you're out." He pointed to the guy pushing the handcart toward the loading dock. "I've taken the liberty of having your belongings packed up. They are waiting on the loading dock for you to claim. Anything not gone by five will be thrown away."

"But Mr. Page. I don't have anywhere to go." Tears ran down her cheeks. She turned toward Derek. "You knew, didn't you?"

He picked up his latte and sipped it. "I did. Thanks for the bonus, Goldie."

She stood in the building's lobby and wept.

Mr. Page got tired of waiting for the keys and told Derek to have the locks changed. When he was off the phone, he stood in front of her and asked if he should get her car.

All she could do was nod.

When he pulled her Acura MDX in front of the building, she walked out with her shoulders rounded in defeat. Derek held his hand out in hopes of a tip.

"You want a tip?"

He nodded. "It would be standard procedure."

Fury and worry bubbled under her skin. "I'll give you a tip. Stop being an asshole." She climbed into her car and drove off. The trip was short since she had to pick up her stuff from the rear dock.

It took her an hour to load the boxes that contained her life. Her mattress was already in the alleyway comforting a homeless man and his dog. Anything else she couldn't fit, she left behind.

Her phone pinged with another message from her site. #where'sTilden.

She knew where he was. She put Aspen Cove into her GPS and started her journey to an uncertain future.

CHAPTER EIGHT

With something akin to a Venn diagram in front of him, Tilden sketched out what he knew about the Carvers and the Coolidges. In the right-hand corner, he made notes of the new information he'd gleaned from Doc.

Ray Bradley was both a Carver and a Coolidge. He chuckled to himself. It was a good thing Abby Garrett never set her sights on him because if what Doc said was true, he and Abby were related. He'd have to do the math, but they were most likely second or third cousins.

He'd always felt odd that Ray left him his estate. While it wasn't a mansion, it was something. Something that sat on several acres of land. A solid structure with potential. If there weren't so many soil samples waiting their turn for testing, he'd have running water in the house.

"You want the usual?" Riley asked. She leaned her hip on the edge of his table, her pad and pen in hand.

"What's my usual?" He raised a brow. Had he become so predictable?

"Blue plate special, coffee black. If you don't look like you're ready to pop at the end, a piece of cherry pie."

"Damn." He wanted to change his order just to prove a point, but Friday was fried chicken night and he loved Maisey's. Just to prove a point that he wasn't as predictable as she believed, he said, "Blue plate special but fries instead of mashed potatoes."

"Living on the edge?" She scribbled the order on the pad and disappeared. It was funny to see her still working here. She'd made quite a name for herself after the benefit concert where Indigo had used her metalwork as focal points on the stage. Word had it that Riley was earning twenty-five grand for most of her larger pieces.

He supposed she was here because of loyalty to her aunt and cousin. They'd taken Riley in when she had little to nothing. Too bad most people weren't as kindhearted.

He scribbled a few more notes and looked

around the diner. Two years ago, if anyone had told him he'd be living in small-town Aspen Cove he would have laughed. He'd been a city boy most of his life.

That was probably his ancestors' plan. They'd get as far away from Colorado as they could without turning back east to their roots. That was how his family had ended up in Sacramento. They ran from the accusations. Ran from the state. Ran from their lives or possibly ran for their lives.

"Here you go," Riley said as she dropped his dinner off.

He breathed in the scent of deep-fried perfection. Cooking wasn't one of his strengths. He had a gas range at the cabin, but it got very little use. Most recipes were designed for family and he wasn't fond of leftovers. That came from his youth when his mother would make a big pot of soup or spaghetti, and they'd eat it all week long. It wasn't until his late twenties that he started eating pasta again.

He lifted a chicken leg and was about to bite into it when the diner door opened and in walked a familiar face.

She scouted out the place as if looking for someone. Each second that passed caused her shoulders to droop farther. When she got to him, it was as if a light turned on and a string attached to her head pulled to full height.

"Hey." She stood tall and offered him a weak smile. Goldie Sutherland was back for more. Too bad he had nothing else to give.

He bit into the chicken, the juice running down his chin to his beard. He didn't acknowledge her, didn't show that he recognized her. She no longer wore a wedding dress. Her lips were a soft kissable pink, not the blood-red he'd had to scrub from his mouth.

Too bad it wasn't as easy to scrub the memory of the kiss from his brain. He'd had two dreams about her in the weeks that had passed. Both of them pleasant. Waking up to a boner brought him back to contraband naked centerfolds and sixteen.

She ambled toward him and when she reached him, she didn't take the seat across from him like she'd done before. This time she waited, as if she wanted to be invited.

"Evening, Goldie."

A whoosh of air rushed from her. "You remember me?" Her voice quivered.

When he looked up at her, he saw a different woman. Weeks ago, she was strong and vibrant and desperate. Today she looked downright beat.

"You're a hard one to forget." He pointed to

the chair across from him. "You want to join me?"

She moved into the red upholstered seat in a flash.

Riley swung by. "Can I get you anything?"

Goldie looked at his plate like a starving animal. "Just water please."

"New diet?"

She frowned. "You could say that. Poverty puts a new spin on things."

He leaned over to look at her outfit. No doubt when she bought it, the money spent could have kept Zachariah in canned stew for years.

He set down his half-eaten chicken leg and wiped his hands on his napkin. "You here to see if I'll give you your money back?"

She laughed, but it wasn't a funny laugh, more of a sardonic one. "No, that money wouldn't make a dent in my life. I've got much larger problems these days."

"And you think your solution to them is here?"

Riley dropped off the water. "You want to introduce me to your friend?" She eyed Goldie with interest.

He didn't have to do anything. Goldie offered Riley a brilliant smile and a handshake. "I'm Goldie."

"Nice to meet you." A group of tourists walked in and took up the large booth in the corner, which sent Riley on a race to get drink orders.

"She seems nice." Goldie lifted her water glass and took a long drink.

"Pretty much everyone here is nice, but that's what you're counting on, isn't it?"

Her eyes grew wide. "What?"

He leaned back in his chair and studied her. This woman was different from the one he'd met before. Those cognac eyes had turned muddy and dull. Her skin was pale. Not porcelain pale, but the color flesh turned when someone was worn out. Even her once shiny hair had lost its luster. It was like someone had reached inside her and ripped out her sparkle.

While his personal policy wasn't to engage in conversation with anyone, he knew she wasn't going anywhere. He needed to get to the heart of this issue because he had chicken that was getting soggy and cold.

"What can I do for you, Goldie?"

"Umm." She picked up the napkin in front of her and twisted it until it tore in half.

"Spit it out. I'd like to eat."

She frowned. "By all means eat. Don't let my miserable life disrupt you."

This was why he wasn't married or had a girl. Women were damn confusing. She came into the diner and interrupted his meal and yet, he was at fault because somehow her problems took precedence.

He did what he knew was smartest. He once had a mom, so he knew how this worked. "I'm sorry. What can I do to help you?"

When she opened her mouth, it was like turning on a tap. "I just thought since you helped me out before you might do it again. Not a picture. I'm well beyond that, although you are getting quite a bit of play on social media. In fact, I should be mad at you because people are more interested in who you are than me." She moved from one thought to the next. "I expected the wedding to boost my career."

"A career based on nothing?" He popped a fry into his mouth.

"It wasn't nothing." She gripped the edge of the table and leaned forward. Her position wasn't to tell a secret but to make a point. "It's exhausting being under a microscope. Everyone looking for a wrinkle or a dimple of cellulite. Who are you wearing? Where can I get it? Pimping shit products online so I can live in a place I don't belong and eat caviar in public but ramen in private."

He sat there and waited for her to finish, but she was a long way from being empty.

"I have a damn bunion from wearing heels. My eyelids start on fire each time I glue those false lashes on. Don't get me started on lingerie. I don't know how girls wear thongs. It's like flossing your ass. Not once but all day long. And those lacy bras, they chafe the hell out of my nips." She shrugged. "Not the La Perla, those are amazing, but who can afford hundreds of dollars for a bra?"

"Apparently you."

"That's the point. I can't afford anything. I never bought any of it. It's sponsored products that I wear, and other people buy them because I say so. The only thing I paid for was rent and sadly I ran out of money for that two months ago." She sagged against the table. "Over the last week, I sold nearly everything I own trying to come up with money so I didn't get evicted. I went to the bank and got a cashier's check for what I had, which was a quarter of what I needed. When I got back to the building with a latte for the asshole—"

"Your landlord?"

"No. Pay attention." She took a quick sip of

her water. "The latte was for the doorman who had been kind to me for the first time in his life. Anyway, I got back and handed the landlord a cashier's check and he asked for my keys." She swiped at her dry cheeks. No doubt by her puffy eyes she was out of tears. "While I was getting a damn latte, they packed up my apartment."

"How far did you go for the coffee? Egypt? Doesn't seem long enough to pack up an entire apartment."

"Have you listened to nothing I've said? I had nothing left. I'd already sold my furniture except for the mattress I had on the floor. It was all a sham. Big beautiful penthouse apartment without a stick of furniture inside."

"Okay, so let's get back to basics. Why are you here?"

"You were nice to me, and I had nowhere else to go."

"You came here for what?" He looked down at his meal. It no longer seemed all that appetizing.

Her expression was unreadable. Her body was stiff. "I need a place to stay, and I have no one else to turn to."

He tried not to react to the fist-like punch to his gut. How could a woman who once had a million followers have no one to turn to?

"I live in a one-room cabin."

She pulled her lip between her teeth and gnawed on it. When it popped free, she said, "Sounds fabulous."

"Are you crazy? You just said you left a penthouse. You party at the best clubs and shop in Cherry Creek."

"How would you know?"

He was ashamed to admit he had looked her up. He went back five years when she was at the height of her career. Funny how popularity could be considered a job. He'd always stayed on the down-low. Maybe that was a learned habit from decades of his family trying to stay under the radar. It's possible they passed that leave-me-alone trait down so no one knew their line held a murderer. Which was something he was set on disproving.

"We have internet here."

"Right, got it just after running water."

He laughed. "That's still coming."

She turned and smirked. "Haha."

"You think I'm joking."

"I know you're joking." She leaned back and crossed her arms, making her breasts lift like an offering.

He shook his head. "Darlin', you definitely don't want to stay with me."

Her lower lip jutted out. It wasn't a practiced move, more of an automatic reaction. "Okay."

He didn't expect her to give up so easily. "Okay?"

She shrugged. "I asked and you said no. I'm learning mighty fast that I can't have everything I want. Hell, I can't have the basic things I need."

Riley swung by and topped off his coffee. "Pie?"

He nodded. He had a feeling he'd need it.

"What was your plan? You stroll in here and hope to find me?"

She cocked her head to the side. The blonde strands fell over her shoulder. "Yes, I hoped I'd find you."

"What would you have done if I wasn't here?"

"Asked around."

"Then what?"

She slapped her hands on the table. "Look, I didn't have a plan beyond finding you and asking you, but I do now."

"Oh please, tell me what it is. I can't wait to hear."

She huffed. "I thought you were a nice guy, but maybe you're not as nice as I assumed, and since I can't stay with you"—she looked over her shoulder and out the window—"I'll march over to the sheriff's station and ask what I have to do to get locked up for the night because I'm not sleeping in my car. It's already down to thirty-five degrees outside."

Riley dropped off the cherry pie and two forks.

He remembered a short time ago he was thinking how much better the world would be if everyone helped each other out.

Goldie's stomach rumbled and she gripped it tightly.

"You hungry?" His voice was soft.

"No."

He slid his chicken plate into the center of the table. "I'm happy to share."

She eyed the thigh or maybe it was the breast. He didn't care. She could have it all if she wanted.

"Goldie, against my better judgment, I'll say yes to your request because kindness is a thing in Aspen Cove."

She flew out of her chair and landed in his lap, hugging him and thanking him. "I take it back. You are a nice man."

"Don't thank me yet." He pointed at the plate closer to her. "Eat up, my place is rustic and brutal."

She took her seat and picked up the thigh.

"You want to talk about brutal? Try fighting the crowds when Macy's has a shoe sale." She bit into the chicken.

Poor Goldie had no idea what was waiting in the woods.

CHAPTER NINE

He said to follow him but how long was he going to drive and to where? Goldie had been in the SUV for over twenty minutes heading into the woods. She'd lost her radio connectivity ten minutes ago, which let her gain some clarity.

She didn't know Tilden Cool. He could be a crazy mountain man. What if he was a serial killer or a closet Hannibal Lector? She was certain she wouldn't taste good charbroiled and served with a glass of Chianti.

More than once she'd considered turning around, but the road was too narrow, and the only way was forward. The tires of her SUV spun in the icy sections, causing her heart to rattle in her chest.

"Maybe a jail cell was the better choice."

As the road wound around, she pictured Tilden's house in the mountains. Would it be an A-frame on a vista? A quaint log cabin tucked into the trees where he sat in front of his fireplace with his yellow Lab at his feet? Would it have a cute clawfoot tub in the corner of the bathroom where she could sink into hot bubbles to unknot the stress of the last few weeks?

As they pulled into a driveway, her heart rose in her throat to choke any response out of her. There was no A-frame. No cute bear carved from a log at his front door. It was a square box erected from crisscrossed logs with mud shoved into the seams. The only thing that gave it any shape or character was the stone chimney that rose from the rooftop.

When he'd said his place was rustic and brutal, she didn't picture this. It was Unabomber creepy.

She put the car in park and laid her head on the steering wheel. "Oh lord. Help me," she muttered. The cardboard box was looking much more appealing at this moment.

Tilden tapped on the glass and startled her. He tugged on the door, but it was locked. She debated putting her car in reverse but then she'd be back in the same boat. Reminding herself she was the one that tracked him down and not the other way around made her feel slightly safer. If anything, she was the creepy one.

With a flip of a switch, she unlocked the door and Tilden opened it to let her out.

"Welcome to my home." He looked over his shoulder at the dark box tucked into the trees. "It's not much, but it's probably better than the cement bench you would have slept on if Aiden arrested you for something stupid."

"Cement? I thought they had cots and blankets." She exited the SUV and closed the door. Anything she needed she could get later.

"Jail isn't the Ritz. I'm sure you'd get a blanket, but the accommodations are built-in."

"Then I'm glad I decided on the Cool Hotel and its five-star amenities."

"Hold your assessment until you've seen the digs."

He led her to the front door, which had no lock. He turned the knob and pushed it open. The hinges squeaked.

"You could oil that."

He chuckled. "It's my alarm." He flicked on a switch and the light flickered to life. "The back door is worse. I'll hear you coming and going."

Her eyes adjusted to the lighting. She had no words to describe what she saw before her. It was her living hell on earth. There was a window on three walls. The same mud shoved into the cracks on the inside as the outside. She walked up and touched it. The texture was rough but solid like cement.

"Mud?"

He shrugged. "I think so, but it could be shit for all I know. It's the same color."

She snapped her hand back and rubbed it on her jeans. Turning in a slow circle, she took in the place. Two walls were covered with bookshelves and books. The only break was the window. One wall had a stove, sink, and cabinets. They were open with stacks of mismatched dishes heaped on top of each other.

Canning jars lined one shelf, while old iron pots and pans filled another. In the corner was a refrigerator that was twice as old as her if the avocado color was any indicator.

Across from her was a door. Since it sat opposite the front door, Goldie assumed it was the back door. To her left was another door she pointed at.

"Is that the bathroom?" She stared down at her hands. She'd either touched mud or poop. Both were gross and she needed to scrub herself clean.

"Yes but ..."

She rushed to open the door. Inside was a bathtub without a spigot, a hole in the floor where a toilet would sit, and a sink that thankfully had everything intact. She rushed over and spun the knobs, but nothing came out.

"You didn't let me finish." Tilden leaned against the doorjamb. "No running water in the place."

Her lower jaw dropped open. "What? You weren't joking?" Her eyes went from the sink to the tub to the hole in the floor. "How do you ..." She lifted her hands into the air. "How do you bathe, brush your teeth, or ... potty?"

"Potty?" He pushed off the frame and walked back into the main room. "Follow me. I'll show you the facilities."

He opened the back door and a breeze whipped around her ankles. She snugged her jacket closed and followed him outside.

"This is the shower." He pointed to a box screened off on three sides. A rudimentary showerhead hung from a pipe tied to a metal post. Above, sitting on stilts sat a metal tank. "You need to fill it up with water from the pump." He pointed to an old-fashioned hand pump that sat about ten feet behind the house. "Throw a few logs beneath the still and light it up. Takes about an hour to heat."

"That's a still, as in moonshine?"

"Yep. Before I got here, Ray gave himself a whore's bath. Bowl of cold water and a sponge. I rigged this puppy up about a year ago." He walked to the right where the last of the sun's rays were sitting. Only a hint of daylight played through the swaying pine needles. "This is the potty."

Goldie stared at the outhouse. It was straight out of a movie with a moon and star cut in the door.

"You should jiggle the handle a few times before you enter so the rodents and snakes move over for you."

Again, her jaw dropped open as if the hinge that held it closed had given way.

He walked over and thumbed the bottom of her chin up to close it. "Just kidding. So far nothing but a bat has been found in there."

"I have to go to the bathroom outside? What am I, a poodle?"

"You could hold it and drive into town to the diner each time, but that seems counterproductive."

She inched toward the outhouse like it was alive. She'd never gone in an outhouse before. Never gone in a Porta-potty, for that matter. When she opened the door and peeked inside, she found a string hung from the ceiling and yanked on it. The space lit up with the bare bulb that swayed above her head.

To her surprise, it was far more pleasant than she'd imagined. Her mind conjured a wooden bench with a hole in it. Spider webs all over the place. A rodent or two cowering in the corner. Instead, it was clean with a toilet seat on a wooden box, a toilet paper holder, a shelf with hand sanitizer and wipes, and a magazine rack that had the latest issues of some outdoorsy looking stuff.

"Where does it all go?"

"It's a self-composting system."

She didn't know or care what that meant. She was still coming to terms with having to walk outside to relieve herself.

When they were back inside, he handed her a bottle of hand sanitizer. "Just in case the walls are poop." He shook the teapot on the stove and turned the burner on below it. "Tea?"

"Where does the water come from?"

He pointed toward the back door. "That pump is connected to a well. No worries, it's safe. I have it checked each year."

Tilden was tall and big. He reached past the canned goods and pulled out two boxes of tea. "I've got mint madness and chamomile."

She moved to the table that sat in the center of the kitchen area and plopped into the nearest chair. The jars of dirt and rocks lined up rattled on the surface. "I've got enough madness in my life. I'll take the chamomile, please."

While he prepped two cups, she took a deeper look at her surroundings. It was an odd mix. A large oversized black leather sectional sat dead center in the room facing the fireplace. It was modern and new. On the back door wall, below rows of books, was a full-sized bed covered in a patchwork quilt that was old but oddly charming.

Tilden brought her a cup of tea and took his to the corner of the living room area, where an old tattered chair sat. He turned on a nearby lamp and kicked up his feet on the ottoman.

Goldie sat there like she was on the outside looking in. This was how he lived. In a one-room shack with an outdoor shower and an outhouse.

She pulled out her phone and scrolled through her contacts. Surely someone else could help her out. Someone who had modern amenities like running water and central heating. She tapped on Sebastian's number, but nothing happened. One glance at her phone told her why. No bars. If she couldn't text an S.O.S. to her friends, then maybe she could chill in front of the TV. She needed some mindless entertainment. Something to distract her from the realities of her life.

"Umm, where's the television?"

Tilden had leaned back as if he were taking a nap. He opened his eyes and looked at her. "No television." He pointed to the bookshelves. "Grab a book."

The tightening of her chest was always the first sign of an impending panic attack. The second was the dizziness, which swept quickly past her. She took several deep breaths to ward off what could be a doozy of a breakdown if she didn't get it under control.

"I don't read books." She sipped her tea, hoping the soothing benefits of chamomile would kick in.

"You're missing out." He rolled from his chair and walked in front of the shelves that would make most home libraries envious. He pulled a book from the stacks and handed it to her. The title stared back at her like it was a foreign language. The letters danced across the hard surface. When one word made itself clear, she said, "I've seen the movie."

"Which version?" He picked up a book for himself and went back to his chair. "I prefer the Colin Firth iteration."

She laughed. Never in her life would she have guessed she'd be sitting in a cabin talking literature and movies.

"I like the zombie one."

"Pure shit." He let out a whoosh of air. "That's the problem. Movies turn great masterpieces into two hours of crap."

"Self-composting crap?"

He shook his head. He pulled a laptop from the side of his chair and opened it. "I've got some research to do. Make yourself at home." He lowered his head to his lit-up screen.

"Wait, how do you have internet and I have no connection on my phone?"

"Different cell tower. Turn it off and then back on or log into my Wi-Fi. It's Tilden with Tilden as the password."

"Very original."

He glanced at her. "I like to keep things simple."

After another look around, she said, "Obviously."

Several minutes later, she had a working phone. For the next two hours she sent out an emergency broadcast, but she might as well have been stranded on a desert island. None of her "friends" were in a position to help.

She waited as long as she could to venture

out to the outhouse. It was coming up at nine o'clock and she couldn't take another minute of her bladder screaming.

She stood at the door for several minutes with her hand on the handle. Peeing in the outhouse seemed far better than peeing her pants, so she shored up her reserve and opened the door.

"Watch out for bears."

"Haha." She marched outside. The last thing she heard was him say was, "I'm serious. It's been a mild winter, and many haven't gone into hibernation." By the time his words sunk in, she was already halfway there. She bolted the remaining distance and slammed the door behind her. There was a latch on the outhouse door but not a lock on the house. How had her life become so topsy turvy?

CHAPTER TEN

Tilden knew he shouldn't, but he couldn't help himself. Ray had done it to him when he first arrived in the woods. The only difference was Ray could make the growl of a bear sound authentic while he could not.

Instead, he snuck around to the back of the outhouse and dragged a branch across the wall. He let out a few heavy breaths and howled at the moon.

"Oh. Hell. No," Goldie said. "I'm not surviving my childhood to be eaten by a bear."

With his hand over his mouth trying to suppress his laughter, he leaned against a nearby tree and waited for her to bolt from the door.

He counted down from three but only got to two when she shot from the outhouse at a full run to the cabin.

He burst into laughter. "You were safer in the outhouse."

She'd raced past him and stopped dead to swing around. "That was you? Who does that?" She marched over to him with clenched fists. "Why would you do that to me?"

"Lesson one in living in the wilderness. Don't run into the jaws of your predator."

She eyed him as if she was determining whether that was him or the wild animal he pretended to be.

"You're lucky I was already finished, or I might have pissed myself."

He kicked off the tree and walked toward her. "I think you're mistaken. You're lucky you didn't wet yourself. It takes at least an hour for the shower to heat." He strode past her to open the door.

"That wasn't nice." She walked inside and collapsed on the sofa.

"No, but it was funny." He poured more hot water into her cup and took a seat in the chair he'd been sitting in before. He didn't pick up a book. Instead, he looked at her. What was she doing in the woods with him?

"You didn't even sound like a bear."

He chuckled. "Good thing, since I was a wolf."

Her eyes grew large. "I have to worry about bears and wolves?"

He stood and perused the bookshelf beside him. When he found the book about Rocky Mountain wildlife, he handed it to her. "This should get you up to speed on the dangers outside."

She stared at it like he'd handed her a turd. "Just tell me what else I'm in for."

He watched her lower lip roll out. He was one step away from seeing if the last kiss was as good as he thought, or if it was because he'd been lonely. She was a distraction he didn't need but he had to admit she was entertaining.

"Sorry, but I don't think there's a movie out, so you'll have to read the book."

She curled into the corner like somehow burrowing in would protect her from the evils of the world.

"I thought you'd be nicer." The cover fell open and she stared at the pages with pictures.

"I let you stay here. I'd say that's nice. It's not the Ritz, but it's warm and dry. Seems to me if you knew anyone nicer, you'd be on their couch instead of mine." He sank back into the old chair and picked up his book. Although he glanced at the pages, he didn't get much read as his attention constantly diverted to her. Each page she turned, her eyes grew wider and wider.

"Snakes and cougars and bears and wolves? I'll get eaten alive?" She stood up and shrugged on her coat. "Thanks, but no thanks." She walked toward the door.

"Where are you going?"

"I saw a refrigerator box outside my old place. I figure if I hurry, I can drag it near a dumpster and call it home until I reinvent myself or find a job."

He set his book down and walked to the door, leaning on it and blocking her exit. "I'm sorry I teased you. Sorrier that I scared you."

He didn't touch her, although he wanted to. Something told him it had been a long time since Goldie had been hugged.

"Stay the night, and we'll figure it out tomorrow."

"You don't even have a place for me to sleep."

He smiled. "I have a bed. You can sleep in it."

She looked between him and the bed. "I let you kiss me and that might have given you the wrong impression."

"You didn't let me kiss you. I kissed you and you kissed me back. The impression I got was you wanted the picture to look real. That was all I was after." He pointed to the mattress. "You sleep on the bed and I'll take the couch."

"Why would you do that?"

"Because despite what you think, I can be a nice guy." He opened a closet by the door and pulled out a sleeping bag. "You need stuff from your car?"

She nodded but stood still.

"Go and get it."

She looked at the door and then at him. "I'm afraid to go outside now."

He took her purse from her hand and set it down before he pulled her in for a hug. "I'm sorry, Goldie. I shouldn't have done that to you."

She stood in the circle of his arms. "I'm sorry to impose on your kindness." She shuddered in his embrace. "I really had nowhere to go."

"Let's get your stuff, and we'll figure it out tomorrow. If you really want a job, I can use a hand delivering some firewood. It's not pretty work, but it's honest work."

She stepped back and looked at him. "I'll do whatever it takes to earn my keep." She lifted on her tiptoes and kissed his cheek.

They made a single trip to her SUV and

grabbed what she'd need for the night and to-morrow. Back inside, they readied themselves for bed. Side by side they brushed their teeth in the kitchen sink using a glass of water to rinse.

When he turned out the lights and climbed into the sleeping bag, he wondered how this woman had crawled into his life and his bed, and he ended up on the sofa?

A SINGLE BARE leg was outside the covers. Long and slim and smooth. The shorts and T-shirt Goldie wore to bed wouldn't be considered sexy by any stretch of the imagination, but the way the comforter flowed over her body, re-leasing just a peek of what was hiding beneath the crazy patchwork pattern made Tilden's blood race hot through his veins.

He never needed an alarm clock. Somehow, he seemed to wake before the sun. It made for productive days. Earlier wood deliveries gave him time to work on freelance projects in the af-ternoon and research his own projects in the evening.

He'd already been outside and filled the still with water and set the kindling ablaze. He figured he'd get cleaned up and set another round for Goldie.

The crisp morning air was always good for a quick wake up. The first heated gush of water he released with the pull of a chord got his blood pumping. Screened off on three sides, the shower opened up to the back of the house. He would have piped it into the actual bathroom if he wasn't afraid of burning down the cabin with the fire under the still.

He sudsed himself up and stood under the heated stream as the water sluiced over his body.

A gasp sounded from the back door.

He whipped around and saw Goldie wrapped in her jacket, those beautiful bare legs peeking from beneath the hem.

Tilden wasn't shy. He stood there naked as the day he was born and watched her eyes eat him up.

"You're next."

She shook her head. "What?"

He pulled the towel off the hook and wrapped it around his waist. "I'll fill the tank for you. Since the fire is hot, it shouldn't take too long to warm the water."

He walked toward her and when he got there, he put his fingers under her chin to raise her jaw. "I'll make the coffee."

She snapped out of it. "Right. I'll ..." She looked toward the outhouse. "Go fend off bears."

"That's my girl." He didn't know why he said it, but he did. She wasn't his girl and never would be. They had nothing in common. They were night and day. Black and white. She was a flower and he was a weed.

He'd half expected to wake up and find her gone. Then again, she had no place to go. He prepped the coffee pot and got it brewing, then pulled clean clothes out of a drawer under his bed. He had to give Ray some credit. Short of running water, the cabin had everything a single man could need.

The *tap tap tap* at the door drew his attention.

"You can come in, Goldie."

She slowly opened the door and stuck her head inside. "I didn't want to catch you dressing."

He laughed. "Why not? You stared at me naked for a full five minutes."

Her cheeks blushed red.

"I did not." She rushed in and shut the door. "It was more like two minutes."

"You got it all memorized." He shrugged on a flannel over his T-shirt.

"Nothing noteworthy to remember."

"Right. Fair enough." He leaned over and pulled a towel from another drawer. "Daylight's wasting. We leave in thirty minutes."

He gave her a quick tutorial on how to use the shower and then came back inside to whip up a few bacon and egg sandwiches.

When she walked inside dripping wet and wrapped in a towel, he almost died. She was gorgeous. Not just in her physical beauty but more so in her vulnerability.

The thing he found most attractive was her trust. He was a stranger and yet, somehow, she'd chosen him.

He laughed when she climbed into the hallway closet to change. He heard her grunting and groaning to move around the boxes and gear stored there.

When she emerged, she appeared more ready for a lunch at the country club than a romp in the woods.

He handed her a sandwich and a coffee and shuffled her outside to his truck.

"What are we doing today?"

"We're delivering wood."

"Oh." She looked at her manicured nails. "No problem."

He had several pairs of gloves in his truck. He plucked a pair out from under the seat and handed them to her. "These should help."

Twenty minutes later they pulled up to Zachariah's house, which resembled a landfill more than a front yard.

He was finishing his breakfast, with more toast trapped in his long gray beard than he got in his mouth.

"I've got three deliveries for ya." Goldie cautiously stepped from the truck. "Who's the bird? You get her from Buttercups?"

Tilden howled. Goldie sold herself, but not for dollars tucked into a G-string. She wouldn't be begging for a place to stay if she had. No doubt she'd pull in some big bucks if her talents lay elsewhere.

"Nope. This is Goldie, and she's helping me out this week."

"I ain't paying extra unless she strips."

Goldie squared her shoulders. "Grandpa, you don't have enough money to see me naked."

Tilden shook his head. "You want to fight or work? One pays better than the other." He didn't have the funds to pay her, but she was in worse shape than him. Tossing some cash her way was the right thing to do.

Given that it was winter, and the ground was frozen solid, it wasn't likely he'd be getting the samples he needed for testing anyway. With the new information he had about mining, the jars on his table would no doubt come back with nothing more than trace metals.

Goldie took out her phone and snapped a selfie with old man Tucker in the background. "No one will believe this."

Tilden hooked up the trailer and waited for her to stop snapping pictures of the various stills.

"Can I post some of these on my website?" She turned to Zachariah.

"Will it bring me business or get you naked?"

"Get in the truck, Goldie." He shook his head at Zachariah. "You'll end up in jail, old man."

"Nah. One of those deliveries is for the sheriff."

When she climbed into the truck, Tilden turned to her. "You still trying to make the social media thing work, huh?"

She shrugged. "Old habits die hard. Besides, this proves I wasn't lying about our marriage." She gave him a wink and took a picture of his profile. "Can I post your picture?"

"Why would anyone want to see me?"

She lowered her head. "Because you're cute."

"But not noteworthy."

He put the car in gear and drove down the dirt road until they hit the highway into town.

Four hours later and they were done. He had to give Goldie credit. She was more than hair dye and acrylic nails. He knew every muscle in her body ached because his did and he hauled wood all the time.

Two of her nails had broken, and the blisters forming on her hands looked red and angry, but she never once complained. Little Ms. Sutherland was more than she appeared to be.

"I just made ten dollars in affiliate income on that damn ugly lipstick." She pointed to the buy link to her signature color. "I posted that it was the perfect color for any event from walks on the red carpet to bootlegging."

He chuckled to himself. Maybe she wasn't more. Wasn't it his mother who told him a leopard never lost its spots?

"Have you ever tried to be honest?"

She leaned against the truck door. "I'm just trying to be a new me."

He'd spoken more to this woman in the last day than he had to the whole town since he'd lived there. What was it about her that made him find his voice? "You mean by being authentic? Why not give them the real you?"

She laughed. "I wouldn't go that far. Nobody wants to see or hear the truth."

Was that the truth, or was it that the truth was too painful?

CHAPTER ELEVEN

People were downright mean. Why did everyone have an opinion or think they were entitled to one? Goldie remembered when her mother would read the reviews for her movies. If they were good, a trip to Rodeo Drive was in the works. They'd dress up and prance around like they were on parade.

If the movie rated poorly, her mother would lock herself in the house and wouldn't come out until a new script arrived and she could try on a new persona.

Liza Sutherland was a method actor. She dove deep into her performances. Goldie never knew who she was coming home to, but she was happy her mother never played a murderess or a child abuser. Life was tough enough being the disappointing daughter of a movie star.

She scrolled through the comments of the video she'd posted last week. It was the one with Zachariah Thomas and his stills. She'd blurred out his face a tad, which made him look better, and posted the picture.

There were only a handful of comments.

No one cares anymore, get a real life and a real job.

You want to impress me? Wrestle with a bear and post that.

Get real Goldie, who wears three-hundred-dollar jeans to chop wood?

She looked at her dwindling numbers and groaned.

"More bad news?" Tilden sat at the table going over maps he'd borrowed from the county assessor's office in Copper Creek. "I guess that means you're staying longer?"

She knew she was a burden to him. There wasn't much she brought to the table with her presence. Hell, she ate his food, took his bed, and sucked up his time.

"I need a job. A real job." He was kind enough to take her on wood runs, but her poor hands were looking like she'd never had a manicure. Her nails had broken so badly she'd had to cut them down to the quick. There wasn't a time in her life where she could remember having nubs for nails.

If her mother could see her now, she'd roll over in her grave. An inch of dirty blonde had grown out from her roots. It had been months since she'd had Botox and the fine lines in the corners of her eyes were appearing. The worry creases that sat like a parenthesis between her brows deepened each day.

"I can put you in touch with Sage. She could use a cocktail waitress at the bar a few hours a week."

She rose from where she'd been lying on the bed and came to sit down across from him. "I don't know how to waitress."

He looked up at her. "What do you know how to do?"

She pulled her lower lip in and chewed. It was the one habit her mother never minded because she said it looked coquettish and gave her lips a boost of sex appeal when they swelled up.

"Nothing. I don't know how to do anything." She laid her head on the table.

"Not true. You've made a living out of manipulating people's perceptions for a long time.

Let's get real, Goldie. You're a beautiful woman, but that's not something you can bank on forever. Be real with yourself, if not your audience."

"You're a chatty one, aren't you?"

He laughed so hard he almost fell off his chair.

She had a hard time connecting the Darth Vader voice to the gentle man in front of her.

"Trust me when I say I'm rarely chatty, but someone needs to talk some sense into you. You can't stay here forever, and you need a job that will pay you enough money to rent a place and feed yourself."

Guilt swirled in her gut like a cyclone. "I'm sorry. I really put you in a bind. How about I take the couch tonight?"

He laid his hands on the table and lifted. "Get your coat, we're going into town."

"I can't go into town with my hair in a ponytail and my makeup willy nilly. What would people say?"

"Probably hello because you look natural and approachable." He stood in front of her and pulled her to her feet. "And beautiful." When he turned her around, he swatted her bottom. "Let's find you a job so you're not moping around the house."

"You think they'd hire me?"

"You won't know until you try."

He shuffled her out the door and into the truck before she could second-guess his actions.

"You want me gone that much?"

"I'd feed you to the bears if I thought I'd get away with it."

In the dying light of the early evening, she could see his eyes sparkle. Somehow, everything she did made his eyes dance with delight—or maybe it was distaste, but either way that little glint never got boring to look at. He never got boring to look at.

"I'm pretty sure the bears wouldn't like me either. Too much filler, not enough fat."

"Now that's getting real. I'm proud of you."

She'd heard that wording a lot today. Get real was obviously the keyword for her life as it stood. "Getting real with Goldie," she whispered.

"What's that?"

She smiled to herself. "Nothing, just thinking out loud." Wanting to change the subject, she turned it back on him. "What is it you're looking for on those maps?"

"Not sure, but I'll know it when I find it."

"You don't have to tell me." She knew he was keeping something tucked tightly to his vest.

Something that meant a lot to him, but he wasn't willing to share it. "But if you're going to preach about honesty, you should practice it."

"Says the girl who pimps out lipstick and eye cream she wouldn't slather on a pig."

"Says the man with a dozen vials of soil on his desk and pretends it's because he likes dirt."

"Observant for the girl who'd rather watch the movie than read the book."

"Arrogant for the man who probably hasn't seen a movie in ten years."

They volleyed back and forth until they reached town. The bar was crowded, and Main Street parking was full, so he pulled behind the building and entered through the back door.

Karaoke night was just beginning.

A man behind the bar saw them come in and looked around. "Not sure there's a seat in the place."

"Indigo coming in tonight?" Tilden asked.

"I hope so or there might be a riot. Dalton says they'll be in later with the band. Everyone is here to finish up the newest album." He pulled the taps and looked at her. "Who's your date?" he asked Tilden.

He placed his hand at the small of her back and moved her forward. "This is Goldie. She's looking for a job." He pointed at the handsome man behind the bar. "That's Cannon." He glanced around the tavern and pointed to a tiny redhead. "That's his wife Sage, who also runs the bed and breakfast and is the nurse in town."

"Wow, she has three jobs. I'm only looking for one until I can get on my feet."

Sage raced to the bar and pulled out three frosted mugs. "Two lagers and a stout." She turned to her. "Goldie Sutherland. I heard you were in town."

Goldie's eyes got wide. "You know me?"

She shook her head. "No, but I plan to." She stared at Tilden. "You're the only one with dirt on Mr. Silent."

She turned to look at Tilden who lifted his brows in an I-told-you-so manner. "You mean Mr. Chatterbox?"

Sage laughed. "No way."

Goldie nodded. "Seriously, he never shuts up." She reached up and pinched Tilden's cheek.

Cannon filled the mugs and set them on a tray. "I'll get these, you train our new employee on how to pull the taps." He glanced at Goldie. "We can pay you minimum wage plus tips."

She had no idea what minimum wage was, but it was more than the pennies funneling into her account now. She'd been in Aspen Cove for over two weeks and had brought in a whopping forty-seven dollars.

"I'm hired?" She cocked her head to the side. "I don't have to fill out an application?"

"No time for that." He tossed her an apron. "Get back here or you'll be fired before you start."

Goldie let out a whoop that drew the attention of the crowd. She tied the apron around her waist and rushed behind the bar.

She glanced back at Tilden, who gave her a warm smile and a thumbs up before he walked toward the pool table.

"You're a godsend." Sage spun in a circle like she didn't know where to start. "What do you know?"

A smile took over her face. "I know I have a job and that color of hair fits you perfectly. You're a spitfire, aren't you?"

"I've been called many things. I'll let you decide."

They washed beer mugs and put them in the freezer below the bar. Then pulled beer from the tap and talked about the perfect amount of head to leave in the glass.

"I know," Sage said, "you'd think men would like all head, but when it comes to beer, less is better."

Goldie laughed. "What about food?"

"I'm the last one to talk to about that." She pointed to the large man who looked like he'd just escaped from jail. "That's Dalton. He brings pizza on Karaoke night. We don't have a kitchen, and it's a good thing because I'm no Julia Child."

"She's more like the opposite of Julia Child. Sage in the kitchen is like asking Hannibal Lector to dinner. No one would live to tell." Cannon grabbed a bowl of mixed nuts and disappeared.

She shrugged, "It's true. What about you, do you cook?"

Cooking was the one thing Goldie could do. She never followed a recipe but made some amazing dishes.

"I love to cook."

Sage nodded toward Tilden, who was taking a shot but looked up as if he knew they were talking about him.

"Are you two a thing?"

Cannon flopped against the counter and asked for four lagers.

Rather than wait for Sage, Goldie pulled the mugs from the freezer and tried her hand at the taps. It was harder than it looked. It required the perfect angle to get it right, but by the second pull, she had it down.

"You're a natural." After that, they left her to her own devices. She moved around the bar and took orders. She had a great memory from all the lines she'd had to rehearse as a kid. Her mother had hired someone to recite her lines to her, so she retained more from listening.

She moved toward a table and found a hand wrapped around her waist. When she was pulled into someone's lap she looked into a pair of blue eyes. "Hey, beautiful. You're new in town."

"I am, but I'm also working. Can I get you something?" She glanced around her. The man whose lap she sat on was at a table with two young firemen still in uniform, but they were drinking soda.

"I'd love a beer and maybe a date."

Before she could reply, Tilden was there. "Hey, Baxter, I can see you appreciate a beautiful woman, but this one isn't available."

He let go of her waist like he'd been burned. "Sorry, man. I didn't know she was taken. You know how it is, finding a single woman in Aspen Cove is like finding a unicorn."

Tilden chuckled. "Be careful of this one. Her horn is sharp."

Goldie jumped to her feet and turned toward Tilden. "You better move, or my horn might find its way up your ass."

He leaned into her and whispered loud enough for only her to hear, "Who knew you were so kinky?"

She pushed against his chest. "Who knew you could be a dick?"

He leaned back. "From what I hear it's unremarkable."

She couldn't help but glance down. "That's not what I said. I said it wasn't noteworthy to remember."

He lifted her chin and planted a chaste kiss on her lips. "But you remember it, don't you?"

She walked away. How could she forget it? Tilden standing in front of her naked with his length hanging heavy against his thigh was not something she'd soon forget. Too bad he was everything she didn't like in a man. He was rough around the edges and dressed like a logger. But he was also kind and hardworking. Then there were those eyes, eyes that could see into her soul. Broad shoulders, deep voice, and his body. Oh, his body was a work of art. Add to that his not noteworthy length and girth. She shook her head. Nope, Tilden Cool was not her type. He was coal and she was an unpolished diamond.

This was the reality of her life. She pulled her phone from her pocket and took a video. "You want it to get real. This is real. This is my life. Starting today," she said in front of the camera. "We're getting real with Goldie."

CHAPTER TWELVE

Tilden sat in silence as he drove Goldie back home. Each time they hit a bump, she groaned.

"Feet hurt?" Was this the first job Goldie had that required her to stand for a shift?

"Everything hurts." She fisted a wad of bills in her hand. It was mostly ones, but she held on to them as if each was a golden nugget. "Especially my pride."

He wove through the back roads with only headlights and the glow of the moon to light the way. When a deer darted in front of his truck he slammed on the breaks.

"Ouch. Are you punishing me?" She rubbed her collarbone where the seat belt had dug in.

"No, I'm trying to get you home alive. A deer crossed the path."

She perked up. "Really? Where?" She twisted in her seat to glace out the back window. "It's gone."

It wasn't his business but there was a lesson to be learned here. "Glad you can see that. Sometimes it's best to look at things in your rearview mirror."

"What's that supposed to mean?"

He pulled into the front of the cabin and parked.

"It means that sometimes it's important to realize the past is in the past and you have to move on to the future."

She unbuckled and opened her door, then rolled out of the car as slowly as a geriatric woman.

He rushed ahead to open the door for her and headed straight for the refrigerator to pull two beers from the top shelf. "You served them all night. You might as well enjoy one. Unless beer is below you."

She tossed the bills in her hand to the bed. They floated like falling leaves to the mattress. "Just say what you want to say. You don't like me?"

"Whoa, this isn't a matter of like or dislike.

It's a matter of reality." He popped the caps off the beers and handed her one. She took it and downed nearly half in her first drink.

"You want to talk about reality?" She spun around. "Look at you. You hole up in your cabin like the Unabomber, only you're not building bombs. You're ..." She pointed at the table and the pile of notes and vials of dirt. "I don't know what you're doing, but from the outside looking in it's weird."

He walked to the corner and flopped into his favorite chair. It was old and tattered and torn but it was comfortable. He'd spent nearly every night for the last two years in that chair reading, editing, or researching.

"You want to talk about weird? How is it you can lie to people all day about who you are and take their money and not feel as if you're stealing from them?"

Her eyes grew wide. "Stealing?" She hobbled to the couch and sank into the cushions. "I've never stolen anything in my life."

He thunked his beer down on the table beside him and watched her for a moment. Her hair was a mess and it had never looked so damn sexy. There wasn't much lipstick left on her lips, which made them even more appealing.

"Each time you post a video about a product you're pimping, you're stealing their trust."

Her lips stretched into a thin line. "How can you say that? I'm merely telling them about a product that they should try. Whether or not they like it is up to them. Whether or not they purchase it isn't my problem."

He kicked out his feet and rested them on the ottoman. "There's where you're wrong. It's all about them purchasing the product because if they don't, you end up in a cabin in the woods living with me."

Part of him loved to spin her up. Over the last week, he'd done it a lot. Her mother might have been a decent actress, but Goldie was a canvas of emotions, and every one of them showed on her face.

"While you're rubbing it in, why don't you work on my aching feet?"

He knew she wasn't asking him to rub her feet, but with the way she had hobbled to the sofa, a good foot rub wouldn't be unwelcomed.

He rose from his chair and sat at the other end of the couch. He tucked his beer between the cushions and reached for her feet.

"What are you doing?" She tugged her booted feet back.

"While I rub it in, you may as well get some

benefit." One more tug and he had her turned around with her feet in his lap. It didn't take long for him to pull off her boots and socks. He wasn't a foot kind of guy. Loved to see a nice pair of legs and never minded a pair of heels wrapped around his waist, but feet weren't his thing. Goldie's were a different matter. They were perfect down to her soft pink polish.

He started with his thumbs at the arch and worked his way to her toes, all while she hummed and moaned. His sixteen-year-old self would have had a hard-on with all the erotic sounds coming from her mouth. His thirty-six-year-old self was finding it hard to keep it soft.

"Back to your business."

A loud sigh whooshed from her lungs. "I have no business."

"Exactly, because you've lost people's trust by lying to them."

She pulled her leg back, but he didn't let her get far. After a few seconds, she relented. The feel of his touch must have been worth the pinch of his words.

"I don't lie."

He shook his head and grabbed his beer for a drink before he continued. "Tell me about one product you advertise that you buy and love."

Her eyes narrowed and her lip twitched to

the side. "There are plenty." She pinched her lower lips between her fingers and twisted and pulled. When it popped free it was pink and puffy and begging to be kissed. He had no idea why he was always thinking about her lips and kissing them.

"I liked the gum I pimped once. It didn't help with weight loss, but the minty taste was good."

"I bet you told everyone it was a fabulous product." His hand moved up and squeezed her leg. "You're naturally slim so I bet the post included a picture of you in skinny jeans."

"How did you know?"

"Because I'm an investigator at heart. I have an inquiring mind, and I wanted to know who Goldie Sutherland was."

"You stalked me." She leaned over and grabbed her beer from the table.

"I prefer to call it research." He sat with her feet on his lap as if they did this every night. "Who was this woman who asked me to marry her? Why did her kiss taste so good?"

She smiled. "It was the weight loss gum."

"Right." She was a mess but a sassy mess that somehow made his drab life more colorful. "Still a lie."

"I didn't lie. I merely stretched the truth."

"Which is a lie. Tell me, who is Goldie Sutherland, really?"

She gnawed on her lower lip for a minute. "She's a nobody. The daughter of a dead movie star. The washed-up who's who of product pimping."

He wrapped his arms around her knees and tugged her closer. Her feet were no longer in his lap, but she sat within inches of him. So close he could feel the heat come off her body.

"When I look at you, I see a woman struggling with her identity."

She adjusted herself so her head leaned on his shoulder.

"You want to know who I am? First, you need to know who I was. I was Liza Sutherland's golden child. Was I golden? No way. Huge mistake. Let me tell you, if abortions were legal back then, I'd never be here. But Mom took the pregnancy and turned it to her advantage. In many ways, I'm a lot like my mom. Apple doesn't fall far from the tree and all. I used you in the same way. Hashtag who's Tilden was more popular than hashtag Goldie. Hell, I think someone made you a social media profile. While your follower numbers are skyrocketing mine are plummeting."

"I've got a social media profile?"

She shrugged. "Yes, and if you want honesty, I created it because there was no way a husband of mine wouldn't have one."

He laughed. "Damn. You'll stop at nothing."

She gripped his arm in a two-handed hug. "I like to eat."

He liked to see her eat. She'd put on a few pounds since she arrived. The extra weight filled in the ghostly hollows below her eyes and sat like a squeezable handful on her bottom.

"Tell me about your dad." His hand wrapped around her shoulder to keep her close.

"I have no idea who he is."

"None?"

She let out a sardonic laugh. "Took it to the grave. I imagine he was some hot soundman on the lot, but I've been told everything from Brad Pitt—who would have been about two at the time—to Clark Gable, who was probably already dead." She sniffled. "Mom milked the mystery for years. She even got a show out of it called "Growing Up Goldie," which was supposed to be a look into my life and my mom as the perfect mother. Don't get me wrong, she was a good mother but like me, she was always trying to make ends meet. Trying to stay at the top of the food chain. She chased youth the way a dog chases its tail." She wiped at her eyes. "You can give me shit for being fake, but it's all I know. I grew up in Hollywood. It's the place where you can be in China and turn the corner on the lot and be in St. Louis in the year nineteen fifty-five. I don't know how to do anything else." Her shoulders shook as silent tears fell.

"Not true." He shifted so he could see her face. "You cocktail waitressed today." He glanced over at the bed and saw it littered with bills. "You made at least forty dollars honestly."

She sucked in a shaky breath. "And my entire body aches, and there's no tub to soak in. Look how far I've fallen. Two weeks ago, I was living in a penthouse and now ..."

"You're living in my house. You have a job that will give you some money to make better choices. Put away the phone and relax into life for a while. I'm not kicking you out. You've got some time to figure it out. Your life will be different. Happiness is not found at the end of a camera lens or on a website. I saw you posting again tonight. What was that about?"

She rubbed her face, leaving streaks of black smudging the rings of her eyes. "It was my inner child fighting back." Another tear ran down her cheek. "Someone said they didn't care about me and if I wanted an audience, I had to get real, so I posted my new reality."

"We all have to face reality at one time or another."

"Tell me, Mr. Wizard, what is it you do that's so honorable?" She pointed behind her to the table. "If I had to guess I'd say you were a spy."

"Calling me a spy is like calling you a movie star. You may perform for the camera, but it's your camera."

"Rubbing it in more?"

"Not at all. I'm making a point."

"Which is?"

"That when you look at me, you see a spy, when in reality, I'm a writer and a historian."

"You're an author?"

He laughed. "I'm no Hemingway, but I have a few books published that help pay the bills." He didn't elaborate because his money didn't come from the sale of his self-published books. He made his money from researching everything from women's clothes in the seventeen-hundreds to ballistics.

"What's that project? Is it a job?" She rose from the sofa and walked to the table. Her hand scrolled across the top of the map. "It's local."

He followed her, leaning over her shoulder and breathing her in. "Yes, there was a dispute between two families in the eighteen-hundreds in these parts."

"Anyone you know? Was it important?"

He shook his head. He didn't know them. "Not really, but because it's local, I'm intrigued. There was a water dispute and a death. Seems mysterious to me, but I keep finding myself at a dead end."

"What were their names?"

He debated on what to tell her, but in all honesty, all she had to do was look at the assessor's maps to see who the land once belonged to.

"Carver and Coolidge." He took his chin off her shoulder.

Goldie, being herself, pulled out her phone and snapped a picture of the table.

She faced him and smiled. "There. It's on your page. One thing I know about people is they're happy to show off. Someone will have some information."

"Goldie ... no. I'm not interested in being a celebrity."

She cupped his cheek. "No chance of that. You need to sell your soul for that kind of exposure. Do you have one, Tilden? You haven't been the nicest man lately, so I'm not sure."

"People still think I'm your husband?"

She shrugged. "I haven't set them straight."

"Lying to people isn't the answer."

"Haven't you ever fibbed?"

He swallowed the boulder-sized lump in his throat. He was the pot calling the kettle black. What would she do if she knew he was a bigger liar than her?

"We're not talking about me. We're talking about you."

"Why is that? Why don't we ever talk about you?"

He knew one way to shut her up and that was to keep her mouth busy. Without another thought, he leaned in and kissed her. This time it wasn't a kiss for show. It was a kiss for purpose. The longer her lips were busy, the less her mouth could open with questions.

His lips lingered for long minutes. Somehow, they'd shuffled from the table to the bed, collapsing on top of the quilt.

He knew he should pull away and tell her to go to sleep, but he'd be damned if he could stop kissing her. She tasted like mint. Probably that damn diet gum she claimed to love. Her body curled into his like it was made to fit all his nooks and crannies. The devil on his shoulder begged for him to push it further. The angel in his heart pulled away.

"It's late, Goldie. Time for bed." He rolled to his feet, taking with him a few of the ones she'd earned. He walked to the kitchen and pulled a canning jar from the shelf. "This should hold your cash."

She rolled to her back. Cheeks flushed and breath labored. "Thanks, Dad."

He licked the taste of the kiss from his lips. "That's just wrong."

She giggled. "That kiss was everything right."

CHAPTER THIRTEEN

It had been a week since the kiss. Each morning she got up, Tilden was already showered and gone. He usually left a note saying he'd be out delivering firewood, or he was in Copper Creek doing research.

She spent her days alone. Even when she lived in the city, she at least was surrounded by people. Out here there was no one when Tilden abandoned her. At least she had a few night shifts at the bar.

How sad was it that the highlight of her day was when a squirrel sat on the windowsill and stayed? How many days had the bushy-tailed creature had to listen to her cry about her life?

Today would be different. She prepped the

still and started the water to heat for her shower. It was already lukewarm so wouldn't take long to get to a toasty temperature.

A dusting of snow had covered the ground, making a hot shower even more appealing. She knew Tilden had heated water for her before he left. He'd been doing that since she'd arrived. The man was a conundrum. He invited her to stay. Kissed her like he liked it, and then ignored her as if she didn't exist.

Each night she lay in bed wondering if he'd ever kiss her again—and if she wanted him to. The answer was a solid yes. Those few stolen moments were the best of her miserable life. How had things gotten so out of hand?

She gathered a towel and the honey shampoo Tilden had given her to use and walked into the cold. After she checked the area for wildlife, she stripped down and climbed inside the shower box. One pull of the string would wash all her worries away. At least for the few minutes it took to clean herself.

It was a process. First, a pull of the string to get wet. A quick lathering and shampooing and then a final pull of the string to release the water to rinse. What once used to be a common everyday occurrence had turned into a thing of beauty. Warm water moving across her body followed by a dry warm towel and a slathering of some kind of honey lotion Tilden had was like a day at the spa.

It was all about perspective. Running water was only a luxury when you didn't have it. A microwave was as valuable as a diamond ring in her book. Tea used to take two minutes on high and now took at least ten minutes, and that was only if the kettle was full. If she had to go to the pump, she needed to add on another five minutes.

She hadn't cooked much. Then again, food was a luxury item. Tilden kept a lot of eggs, bacon, and bread on hand. There was never a shortage of hotdogs and buns either. As she lay on the bed to button her once loose pants, she considered herself lucky instead of fat.

The most frustrating part of her situation was that she'd put herself here. She'd seen firsthand what happened when a person let others dictate their life.

"Mom, if you were here, I'd hug you before I turned you around and kicked you in the bottom."

She waited a few seconds to see if her mom would answer. Sometimes she heard her in the recesses of her mind. The messages were always silly things like *Don't wear white after Labor Day* or *Clamp down your molars before you smile for a picture. It will firm up the parts under your chin.* There was never any real wisdom to the words. Or maybe there was. In remembering her mother, she found the truth about herself. She was a vapid wastrel of human flesh.

"No more." She thought back to her first night at the bar. Hadn't she posted about her reality? No one cared, but something about being honest with herself was freeing. She'd always used her social media status for money, but what if she used it for something else? What if she used it as a way to vent her fears and come to terms with her existence?

Once again, she was most likely lying to herself. Deep down inside there was still a smidgen of hope that her followers would show interest.

For the second time in as many weeks, she turned the camera around and posed in Tilden's chair with a book in her lap. She walked to the stove holding the teapot. She even ventured outside to the outhouse, but nothing looked real because it wasn't. In her attempt to get real, she'd prepared every scene. Placed every prop. This was worse than before.

The tears fell freely. She stomped outside and turned the camera on herself once more.

"You want real?" She scanned the land

around her. "This is real. This is what my life has become. You want to know where Tilden is? I have no idea. He kissed me the other night and I've seen little of him since."

She wiped at the tears rolling down her cheeks before she flipped the camera toward the outhouse, then back to herself.

"I'm a fraud and a phony." She walked the path into the forest until she came upon a clearing with a flat boulder. Seated, she looked into the lens. "I'm thirty-two. Wear a size eight and not a four." She lifted her jacket to show her unbuttoned pants. "Scratch that. With all the bacon and egg sandwiches Tilden cooks, I'm probably a ten." She set the phone in her lap and looked down on it. It wasn't a great angle. It didn't flatter her features one bit, but it was real. "I lived in a castle in Denver until my life fell apart."

She was silent for a few minutes. It wasn't until her phone dinged with an incoming message from her blog that she realized she'd forgotten she was recording.

"Who's Tilden," she continued while shaking her head. "I have no idea who he really is, but I know he's a good guy. He took me in when I had nowhere to go. He's not my husband, but he's become my friend, and I'm grateful to have one in this world." She looked around to see a bird sitting on a bare branch staring at her like she'd lost her mind. Maybe she had. Only an idiot would talk to squirrels and tell the universe her real age. "You want real? Tune in from time to time, and I'll show you real. It won't be pretty, but it will be authentic." She blew the phone a kiss. "I'm not selling you anything, I'm giving you the down and dirty, the brutal truth."

She turned off the video and tucked her phone inside her back pocket. It continued to beep with incoming messages. On her feet, she made her way back to the cabin. Half of her wanted to see what people were saying. The other half told her to let it go. She'd faced enough truths today. If anyone else was mean to her she'd never recover.

What she needed right now was comfort food. With her keys in her hand and a few dollars pulled from her jar she climbed into her SUV and headed toward town. There was a plate of French fries calling her name and if she was still feeling down, a muffin from the shop across the street should do the trick.

When she got to Aspen Cove, she skipped the fries and went straight for the muffin.

A blonde was behind the counter stocking the trays of the bakery when she walked inside.

"Hey, Goldie. I was wondering when you'd come in for a treat."

She looked behind her to see if maybe there was someone standing there. "You know me?"

"No, I know of you." She wiped her hands on an apron that read, *Classy, Sassy, and a bit Smart Assy.* "My name is Katie and Sage is my bestie. She says you're working at the brewhouse."

"They were nice enough to give me a job."

Goldie walked the length of the display case taking in the muffins, brownies, and cookies.

"First one is on the house."

She smiled. This small-town thing was rubbing off on her. It was nice to have someone know her as more than Liza's daughter, or the girl who lived in a penthouse apartment, or the face that froze in time. Nice that she could walk inside a place and be offered something because she was there.

Tilden accused her of using people to buy products, but it was a two-way street. She got used a lot because of who she was and what that little bit of notoriety could bring.

"I'll have the apple spice muffin."

Katie plated it up. "You want a coffee?"

"You have coffee?" She'd become a tea drinker at Tilden's because the percolator was too hard for her to figure out and the only other option was instant.

"It's just the pods, but if you ask me, they're all right. I'll take that as a yes?"

"Yes." She could use a cup. It was Saturday and her final shift of the week. What a blessing Sage and Cannon had become. Despite it being winter, the brewhouse stayed busy all the time. An extra treat was meeting Indigo, or Samantha, as everyone called her. It was funny to Goldie that the popstar could blend seamlessly into the small town. If she could do it, then Goldie could acclimate.

"How are you liking Aspen Cove?" Katie walked around the display case carrying a steaming cup of coffee and a plate with a brownie and a muffin. "You looked like you could use a little more than a muffin."

"It's that obvious, huh? What was it that gave me away? The bags under my eyes or something else?"

"I recognize the fish out of water. I'm not from here either. I'm a Texan born and raised."

"Really? What brought you here?"

She pulled out a chair under a corkboard called the Wishing Wall and took a seat. "A little pink envelope brought me here, but Bowie made me want to stay."

She sat across from Katie and pulled off the top of the muffin and chewed. It was an explosion of spicy sweetness. "So good."

"Bea's recipe. I never met her, but she made all of this possible because she had faith in the people of this town. What about you? What's your plan? Are you staying or is this a stop on your path?"

"Funny thing is, I ended up here because Tilden was kind enough to take a picture. Just goes to show you that kindness isn't always a good thing. The poor man was nice and look at where it got him. I'm sleeping in his bed and he's sleeping on the couch."

"He doesn't seem too unhappy about that. Then again, how would we know? He's not very talkative."

She'd heard that a lot. "I think I may be with a different Tilden. Everyone describes him like he's mute, but I'll tell you, he never seems to be at a loss of words around me."

Katie laughed. "Maybe you bring out the best in him."

"Or ... maybe the worst. He's been kind of avoiding me. I think I've worn out my welcome. Probably time to find a full-time job and a place of my own."

"You don't sound all that enthused."

She shrugged her shoulders. "Everything is new to me and Tilden is ... well ... he feels like home."

"Sounds to me like you don't want to move."

"I don't, but I also don't want to be a burden to a man who was kind to me and opened his life and home to me."

Katie leaned back in the chair and rubbed her chin. "I own the apartment above the bakery. It's two bedrooms and only one is occupied right now. I'll ask Baxter if he minds if you move in."

She shook her head. "Oh no, I wouldn't want to impose. Besides, I'm not sure I could afford the rent."

"It's free. Everyone can afford free."

"Did you say Baxter?" She remembered the man who'd wrapped his arm around her waist and pulled her to his lap her first day on the job.

"Yes, he's Riley's brother, Maisey's nephew and Dalton's cousin."

Tilden had told him she was taken when Baxter showed interest. He'd even pressed a chaste kiss on her lips as if claiming her. Was he jealous? Making Tilden jealous gave her a spark of joy. She liked him more than she wanted to admit. Was it possible that he liked her too and his absence was him distancing himself? Who was he trying to protect? Him? Her?

How long had it been since she'd been in this position? Figuring out whether a man liked her was more fun than finding out where her next meal was coming from.

"That would be great if you could ask him. I wouldn't want to be a burden to anyone. I'd be happy to pay rent."

"I'll let you know tonight. You're pulling beers at the brewhouse, right?" The sound of the oven timer beeped, and Katie rose from her seat. She pulled a pen and sticky note down from the corkboard. "While you're at it, fill out a wish. You never know how things will turn out. Aspen Cove no doubt has a few surprises in store."

Goldie sipped her coffee and ate every crumb from her plate. She stared at the Post-It and the pen. There were a thousand things she could wish for. This year's Prada bag came to mind but where would she use it? World peace and ending world hunger were two that she could jot down but this wasn't about the whole picture. This was something different. It had to come from her core. From the tiny place in her heart that still believed that wishes and dreams could come true.

She thought long and hard about the wish. She wrote several but crossed them out.

~~A full-time job.~~

~~A place to call home.~~

~~An escape from my dismal life.~~

Nope, there was only one thing she wanted.

She wrote *One more kiss*.

The first was for her benefit. The second could have been an accident. But if there was a third then she'd know there was something between her and the bearded mountain man who had caught her when she was falling.

She folded the note and stuck it in the envelope. She laid a five-dollar bill on the table and shouted goodbye to Katie, who had gone into the back room. When she left the bakery, a sense of peace flowed over her. She'd been honest with her audience. She'd been honest with herself. The next question was ... could she be honest about her feelings for Tilden? Would he be honest about his for her?

CHAPTER FOURTEEN

Sidling up to the bar on a Monday evening was out of character for Tilden, but he'd missed his normal weekend visit because Goldie was working. He told himself it was because he didn't want to distract her, but the truth was he couldn't be there and watch the single men of Aspen Cove move in on what was not his, but somehow felt like his.

He'd had no business staking claim to her the last time when Baxter flirted and asked her out. All he was missing was a loincloth and a wooden club for his caveman persona.

The slap of a napkin and a mug of beer pulled him from his thoughts.

"Thanks, man." He took the first sip and savored the bitterness of the hops.

"Not your normal night. You hiding?" Cannon reached under the bar and brought out a bowl and a container of bar snacks. He poured a healthy serving and set them in front of him.

"Who would I be hiding from?" Tilden picked out the spicy peanuts and lined them up. When they were gone, he separated the round crackers from the square crackers.

"Tall blonde with eyes the color of whiskey, a smart mouth, and a phone that never gets a rest?"

"Don't know her." He smiled as he popped a few crackers into his mouth and washed them down with a long draw of beer.

"You'd be the only man in town who doesn't. She's like a bee and every guy within a ten-mile radius is a flower hoping to be pollinated."

"What? Who's Goldie trying to pollinate?"

Cannon chuckled. "Don't know the woman sleeping in your bed, huh?"

"She isn't sleeping with me. That kind of intimacy requires more information. All I'm saying is I don't care what she does."

He wiped the bar down and came back to stand in front of him.

"How hard is it to lie to yourself?"

He raised a brow. "I don't know, Cannon.

You tell me." He rearranged the crackers so they alternated between round and square in a single row.

"Because I did it, that makes me an expert and from where I stand, I'm seeing something a lot different than what you're selling."

A group of guys came in and took the corner table.

Tilden didn't know them but knew of them. They had finished Luke and Riley's house on the beach and were back in town to pick up their equipment. If he'd had the money, he would have hired Cooper Brothers' construction too. They could erect a greenhouse in record time. The only thing green in Tilden's life was his streak of jealousy. It was ridiculous how Goldie could spin him up.

Just listening to her breathe at night made him hard. He hadn't even taken hot showers the last week because the ice-cold water was the only thing that could turn his mind and body away from the damn kiss they'd shared. A kiss that shouldn't have left him wanting more.

It was supposed to shut her up. That was its only purpose. He wasn't ready to tell her his secrets.

Why was that?

His logical mind said it was because she'd

post it on her social media, but his heart knew it was because he didn't want her to know that possibly he shared DNA with a murderer. His family had lost everything because of that accusation. He didn't want to lose what little he had from the same truth or lie. He'd come clean once he had the facts.

"Top it off?" Cannon asked.

"Yep, and then I'm out of here." The brewhouse closed at eight on Mondays. He couldn't say he blamed Cannon for wanting to get home to his wife. She worked during the day and he worked most nights.

"Going home to Goldie?"

"I'm going home." His heart lurched. Knowing she was there made him want to hurry. Then again, what was the point? All they had in common was a few amazing kisses.

"Just fess up. You like her."

He was tired of fighting it. "Yes, I like her, but I don't know much about her. Nothing about her is real, from her hair color to her breasts."

"You've seen them? Touched them?"

He hated to admit that he'd copped a quick feel during their last kiss and they felt real.

"No ... well ... maybe a quick feel."

Cannon tossed his towel on the table. "I

knew it. You guys are a thing." He pulled out his phone and sent off a text.

"Who are you messaging?"

"Sage. She owes me five bucks."

"You're betting on my love life?" He tossed a cracker at Cannon that bounced off his chest to land back on the bar.

"She said you're not a thing, but I know the look a guy gets when he's into a woman. The last time you were here, you stared at her like she was a bone and you were a dog."

"Geezus, Cannon. Goldie isn't a bone. She's a beautiful woman."

"Can you say that again so I can record it?" He held up his phone. "Sage won't believe me. She says if you guys were a thing then Goldie wouldn't be moving in with Baxter."

"She's what?" He picked up his beer and drank it down. "When did this happen?"

"I guess sometime during the week when you were pretending you didn't like her."

"Shit." He tossed a ten on the counter and walked out.

For a few minutes, he sat in his truck wondering if he were too late. Had he messed everything up with Goldie, including their friendship? He would have called her, but they'd never exchanged numbers.

Now he felt bad for ignoring her the last few days. He had no idea what she was thinking. Hoping to get a clue where her headspace was, he pulled up her blog but was redirected to a vlogger account named Getting Real with Goldie.

There were two posts. The first was her starting day of her new job. The second was recorded two days ago. He watched it twice before he put the car in gear and raced home. All the way there he took the imaginary club and beat himself over the head with it.

She'd gotten real all right. She'd spilled her heart out to a small audience. She'd confessed everything from her age to her weight.

The tears streamed down her face as she told them how growing up in Hollywood wasn't as glamorous as they would believe. Confessed to lying about the marriage to save her career. Her words replayed in his head. "Who's Tilden? I don't know who he is, but I know he's a good guy. He took me in when I had nowhere to go. He's not my husband, but he's become my friend, and I'm grateful to have one in this world."

"Fine friend I turned out to be." He took the dirt road faster than he should have. Each dip and bump seemed twice as deep or twice as high. Every one of them wracked his body.

All he could think about was how hard he'd been on her. He'd basically taken a kitten and thrown her into a den of wolves.

When he pulled in front of the house, relief washed over him because her SUV was there. Half running, he burst through the door to find her making the bed. Her small suitcase and handbag sat on the floor next to the door. Everything he saw told him what Cannon had said was true. She was leaving him. Although they weren't a couple, it felt like this was a breakup.

"It's true? You're leaving me for Baxter?" He would have loved to have spewed a list of flaws about the man, but he couldn't come up with one. He was sure there were many but because he didn't socialize, he hadn't talked to Baxter much.

"Leaving you?" She turned around and went back to making the bed. "I thought you'd be relieved."

He stepped forward. Everything inside of him shook. "Why would I feel relieved?" He moved one slow step at a time toward her. There wasn't a plan for when he got there, but he was certain it would include his lips against hers.

"Now you can come home. No more staying away to avoid me." She fluffed the pillows and placed them at the head of the bed. "I've washed the linens and the towels." She looked over her shoulder to where a stack of clothes sat folded on the coffee table. "I didn't think you'd mind if I washed your dirty laundry. It's the least I could do for your hospitality."

"Stop. You don't have to leave."

She spun around to face him. Red rimmed her eyes. It reminded him of the day she'd shown up at the diner hungry and in need of a place to stay.

"I do, Tilden. I really do."

"No, you don't." He reached for her, but she evaded his touch.

She moved to the kitchen area, where the dishes sat drying on a towel. "I was hoping to get this all done before you got back. I guess I misjudged the timing."

"Why are you doing this? I told you to stay."

She placed her favorite tea cup on the shelf and folded the towel and set it on the counter. "That should do it." She looked around and when she glanced back there were tears jeweling in her eyes. "Thank you. You'll never know what your kindness meant to me."

He stood there and stared at her for a moment. "Why are you leaving me?" His voice was raw.

She swallowed hard like a lump was caught

in her throat. "Because ..." She swiped at the tears that rolled down her cheek.

He moved toward her, setting his hands on her shoulders. There was a moment when he thought she'd fall into his chest. He imagined his arms wrapping around her before he covered her mouth in a kiss.

"Tell me what's wrong."

She shook her head. "You and me. It's all wrong. My self-esteem is at an all-time low. My self-worth is bankrupt. I can't have you making me feel like something when you kiss me and then you pretend it didn't happen. Each time you walk away from me I become less. When you destroy what little bit I have, I'm left with nothing. Less than nothing." She shrugged him off and walked toward the back door. "I need a minute and then we can say goodbye."

He followed her to the door, but she turned around and pleaded, "Give me a minute, please." He closed the door and walked to his favorite chair and sank into the tattered upholstery. His eyes watched the clock on his phone. He'd given her five minutes and she still wasn't back.

If her belongings weren't still at the door, he would have thought she'd left already. How long could she spend in the outhouse sulking?

When another five minutes passed, he went

outside to knock on the door and coax her out, but the door was open, and she was nowhere in sight.

His heart dropped like a falling star. How many times had he told her not to go far after dark because it was dangerous? There were a dozen things that could be out there waiting for her and none of them good. Uneven ground that could send her falling. Low branches that could mar her pretty face. Cold temperatures that would soak into her bones. Those were the best of the worst. It might be winter but there were animals that didn't sleep through the frosty months.

"Goldie!" he called. He listened as silence answered him. "Damn woman!"

He jogged inside and grabbed the handgun Ray had left him and his coat and set out to find her. Ten minutes later he broke through the edge of the brush and his heart halted.

She was there sitting on a boulder. "Stop trying to scare me, Tilden. I know it's you." She brushed her hand at the space on her neck where the heat of the animal's breath caressed her. "You're not even good at growling."

He tiptoed forward, hoping he didn't startle the wolf. All it would take was one bite and she'd be down.

"Goldie," he said as calmly as he could. "I'm right here. Don't panic."

Behind her, the wolf growled as if protecting a bone. Tilden's bone and he wasn't of a mind to share.

"Tilden?" She stared at him with eyes as round as the moon. "Oh, God."

With his heart in his throat, he raised the gun and moved forward. It took every bit of effort he had to keep his voice steady and calm.

"Don't make any sudden movements."

She froze and became as still as the stone she sat on.

He wasn't sure if he should raise the weapon and fire or lunge for Goldie hoping to frighten the animal away. More often than not, they traveled in packs and yet this one seemed to be alone, at least for now. No doubt the wolf would have howled once dinner was served, but there was no way Goldie would be its next meal.

"When I count to three, you will fall to your right. Got it?"

He didn't wait for her to acknowledge.

"One. Two. Three." When she rolled to her right, he lunged forward and shot into the air the first time and pointed the handgun toward the wolf the second, but pulling the trigger was unnecessary. In a split second, the beast had disappeared into the woods.

He raced to where she lay curled into a ball. After tucking the weapon into the back of his belt, he scooped her up and carried her back to the cabin. She didn't cry. Didn't move at all except the unintentional shudders that ran through her body.

That scared him more than anything else because Goldie was never silent. In the weeks since she'd been there, quiet had been a luxury he wasn't afforded. She prattled on about everything from the traffic in Denver to the way the air outside smelled of pine needles and hope. He didn't know what hope smelled like. With her in his arms, he would have argued it smelled like spun sugar and cinnamon, which was how she always smelled to him.

"You're okay," he whispered against the top of her head. "I've got you."

She gripped the fabric of his shirt and the silent shudders found their voice with a whimper. He pushed through the back door of the cabin and took her straight to the bed, where he laid her down on the quilt. He pulled it over her shaking body and sat on the edge. Her hands reached for him and once again she held on to the fabric of his shirt as if it were a lifeline.

"He was g-g-oing to eat me." She rolled into him and buried her face into his lap.

With gentle strokes, he rubbed her back. "I've got you."

She sucked in uneven breaths. "You saved me again."

"There was no way I would let him get a bite." It was good she was talking. This situation could have turned out so differently. Worst case scenario, she could have been attacked, or she could be in shock, which was still a real possibility if he couldn't get her calmed down and warm. "Let me get you some tea."

"No," she cried. "Don't leave me."

He looked down at her and all his resolve to stay away was gone. How could a person avoid the light for the rest of his life? Goldie was like the sun in his otherwise gloomy existence.

He shifted her body and lay down beside her, pulling her into his arms. She fit perfectly. He held her close, hoping the heat of his body would warm the chill in hers.

It took her about fifteen minutes to stop shaking. Another five to fall asleep.

He slowly moved himself away and pulled every pot he could find from the shelves and fired up the stove. He snuck outside and lit the still. Tonight, Goldie would need a hot bath and a glass of wine.

She wouldn't sleep for long. He knew the fitful slumber she was in now was because her body had given up for a few minutes.

He hoped she would stay asleep long enough for him to prepare what he knew she needed. He hadn't given it much thought, but she was out of her element living in the woods. She wasn't made of the tough stuff it took to live off the grid.

Hell, it took him six months before he got used to his life here in Aspen Cove. Back in Sacramento, his evenings were filled with a stop at Rendezvous, his favorite bar, before heading home to grade papers. While he didn't have a regular girlfriend, he had a few hookups—women who weren't looking for anything but a good time. He was all about having a good time.

Sadly, he hadn't had that kind of fun since he moved here. Partly, it was because of his focus on his family legacy, but the other reason was the lack of single women in Aspen Cove. Add to that his quiet demeanor and it was a perfect recipe for lonesomeness. He hadn't realized how isolated he'd become.

He should have recognized how dire the situation was when he was willing to sit in the diner for hours on end just to be part of something.

Bucket after bucket of boiling water made it to the tub. He hoped it wouldn't cool too fast. When she woke up, she'd be sore from all the shaking and stiffened muscles. He wanted to give her a little bit of her former life. A life that no doubt included spa days and wine.

He dug through the closet in search of the beeswax candle Abby had given him. He lit it and set it on the ledge of the tub next to a glass of chardonnay.

He looked around the bathroom and smiled. This was how his life should be. Running water. Inside showers. A bath filled with steaming water and scented oils. Soft towels. Wine. Candles. A beautiful woman to share it with.

He walked to the edge of the bed and sat.

"Goldie, sweetheart." He rubbed his palm over her hair and brushed it from her face.

She woke with a start. "Don't leave me." She moved as close to him as she could without crawling into his body.

Something fierce and protective had taken over when he saw she was in danger. Something feral and possessive crept inside him.

"I'm not leaving you."

"But you did."

Had she noticed he was gone? "I was running you a bath."

"No, you left me all week. You avoided me."

He couldn't deny it. He'd done everything he could to stay away from her because everything in him wanted to be so close and he didn't understand it at all. They had nothing in common. Absolutely nothing.

"I'm sorry. It's just that ..."

"You don't like me. I get it. I'm hard to love."

"No, that's not it at all." He rubbed his face with his free hand. "I like you, Goldie, and that ..." He let out a long sigh. "That might not be good for either of us."

She nodded. "I understand."

He shook his head. "You couldn't possibly understand." How could he tell her he wouldn't offer a tarnished reputation to anyone? Especially her. Her life was built on a house of cards that was already tumbling. He wouldn't be the reason the whole thing crumbled.

"Did you say bath?"

"Ah, there's my girl." He stood and took her hand to pull her to her feet. When she stood, her knees buckled. "Steady." He scooped her up and walked her to the bathroom.

"You said there was no running water." She squirmed in his arms. "Tilden Cool, if you lied to teach me a lesson, I'll feed you to the wolves." At the mention of wolves, her body shuddered again.

"No lies, there isn't any running water. While you rested, I boiled water so you could have a bath."

She looked around. "Candles and wine too. Is this a seduction?"

He chuckled. "I hadn't thought of it like that but seeing it through your eyes, I get why you'd ask." He set her on her feet. Since she was still unsteady, he leaned her against the wall and started to remove her clothes. "This isn't sexual but medicinal." He pulled her shirt over her head and tossed it to the floor.

He took in her milky white skin and her pink lace bra.

"Why is that? You kiss me like you like me, but you keep your distance." Her palms rested flat against his chest. Her chin lifted so she could look up to his face. "Did you like kissing me?"

He nuzzled his beard into the crook of her neck while he reached around to unfasten her bra.

"Very much. Your mouth was made for kissing."

She let her hands skate down his cotton T-shirt until her fingers rested on the waistband of his jeans.

"I think you kissed me to shut me up."

"You're right. Do I have to do it again?"

She dropped her head and leaned it against his chest. "Maybe."

He stepped back and her lacy bra fell forward to reveal small but perfect breasts with pebbled rose-colored pearls begging for attention.

"This was a bad idea." He shifted his weight to ease the tightness in his pants. "Are you steady enough to finish undressing yourself?" Whatever made him think undressing her was a wise move was, in fact, stupid. Not a day went by that he didn't wonder what was under those clothes. He'd caught glimpses of her from time to time. Moments when the bedding slipped off her shoulder and he caught the curve of her breast, or on the nights she slept with a bare thigh out of the blankets.

"I don't think so." Her voice was soft but playful.

"I think you're recovered." He broke away from her and stepped back.

Her eyes shifted around the room. "Please don't leave me." She stared into the dark corners. "I'm afraid."

He breathed through his nose and out his mouth, hoping to gain some strength. All he wanted to do was push her against the wall and kiss her. That was only the start. He could almost feel that rose-colored bud between his lips. The feel of her naked breasts filling his palms. He was falling into the abyss already and her jeans were still on.

"Water is cooling down so let's get you in the tub." He lowered his hands to the button of her pants and unfastened and unzipped them. He looked the other way when he pulled them down her legs but realized he'd forgotten to remove her boots. On his knees with his eyes at the perfect height to take in her matching lace underwear, he sent a silent prayer to the gods to give him strength.

When she was standing in nothing but a swatch of cloth, he put his lips right next to hers. "Please don't make me take them off. I'm just a man. A weak man."

She giggled and wiggled out of the lace panties, letting them drop to the floor.

As much as he told himself not to look, he couldn't help it. His eyes went straight to her rounded hips, the curve of her thighs and the trimmed blonde thatch of curls between her legs.

"Get in the tub now." He was out of willpower. He had nothing left in his reserves. If she made one move toward him, she wouldn't be spending the next hour soaking in the tub. He'd have her pressed to the mattress with him buried inside her.

Against his better judgment, he watched her climb over the edge. A turn of her body gave him a glimpse at her backside. All he wanted to do was drop to his knees and bite the perfect globes of her ass. Instead, he turned and walked to the door.

"You relax. I'll boil more water."

He rounded the corner before he heard her.

"Tilden? You can join me if you want."

On the other side of the wall, he leaned face-first into the wooden logs and pounded his head against the wood.

"Goldie, you have no idea what you're asking for." The water sloshed and her giggle echoed through the cabin.

"No, but after my near-death experience, I know what I want."

He filled a pot with water and let her stew on her statement. Did she know what she wanted? Was it him?

"Be careful what you ask for. You might get more than you were betting on."

She laughed. "God, if a girl could get so lucky."

When the water started to bubble, he lifted a pot from the stove and entered the bathroom.

She was like a goddess by candlelight. The light of the flames danced off the white wall. The blondest parts of her hair appeared to sparkle and her once pale skin was flush with color.

The water skimmed the tops of her breasts. She was beyond beautiful and he knew right then if he didn't turn and leave, he wouldn't be able to.

"Pull your legs back so you don't get burned."

When she did, he dumped the hot water into the bathtub. "Feel good?"

"You'd know if you joined me."

He shook his head and backed his way toward the door. "It's starting to snow. I'm going to gather firewood so you stay warm tonight." He dashed from the bathroom.

His hand was on the backdoor handle when he heard her ask, "What's wrong with me that makes you run?"

Not a damn thing and that's the problem. He gathered wood and started the fire. His body was screaming for relief, but his head was telling him to tread carefully. Goldie was at a vulnerable time in her life, and he didn't want to be another bad decision on her list of many.

At the creak of the floorboard, he turned to see her walking toward him in nothing but a towel. When she got to his side, she let the towel drop and fell to her knees beside him.

"No strings attached. Just the comfort of each other's bodies for one night. Will you turn down what I'm offering you?"

CHAPTER FIFTEEN

She was putting herself out there. Every single wet inch of her body. The wolf breathing down her neck was a wake-up call. Life was too damn short to not take chances.

This was a bad decision, but she wanted to feel something other than self-loathing and fear. They were two consenting adults. Why couldn't they enjoy each other? Why shouldn't they?

"I'm not asking you to love me, Tilden. I'm asking you to make me feel something other than despair. My life is a shit storm. Can't you be my safe harbor for a while longer?" That's what he'd turned out to be. Little did he know when she showed up dressed like a princess on steroids, he'd wind up being her unsuspecting prince.

"You're chipping at my resolve, Goldie. I'm trying to stay strong for both of us."

She shuffled on her knees to get closer to him. Her breasts pressed into the soft, worn cotton of his shirt. He closed his eyes and breathed through his nose.

"Do you have any idea what you're getting yourself into?"

"No. Don't care." She gripped at the hem of his shirt and pulled it up and over his head. She'd seen his body. Devoured him for an entire two minutes that day staring at him in the shower. As her fingers moved over his skin and goosebumps danced under her touch, she didn't care what she was getting herself into. All she knew was that she wanted more.

When her lips touched his collarbone and his breath hitched, she knew she'd won a game she hadn't intended to play. He claimed that the bath, wine, and candles weren't intended for seduction and, knowing Tilden like she did, she believed him. Everything he'd done for her was an act of kindness.

He'd had ample opportunity to take advantage of her, but he never did.

However, she had seduction etched into her mind when she let him undress her. When he planted the idea of more. When she let the towel fall to the floor. Everything she did was with the end result in the forefront of her mind. Tilden Cool was one hot-blooded man who made her insides coil with need. One of his smiles could make her heart race for an hour. One of his kisses turned her bones to gel.

Not once in her life had she dated a man like him. Wouldn't have given him a second glance if he were walking on the street. That was part of her problem. She knew what she knew. She did what she did because it was all she knew. Her life was shit because she fell back on old habits and never gave something fresh a chance. Everything in her life was a jumble. Each moment was a risk. Wasn't it time she reached past her comfort zone?

Her mother always told her to order salads because you couldn't get fat or go wrong with lettuce. She said to trust no one because your best friend would trip you just to get first in line at an audition. She also said to wear black because it was a safe color. But Goldie was tired of playing it safe. Safe hadn't worked out all that well with her.

"Kiss me," she begged, and he did.

His mouth crashed over hers with so much force they fell to the floor together. In seconds her naked body was on top of his mostly clothed one, but she didn't care.

Tilden wasn't the kind of guy that threw caution to the wind; he had to have his layers pulled back one at a time.

As long as his mouth was on hers and his hands were exploring, she could wait a few more minutes.

He lifted her up. She hung like a rag doll over him.

"You asked for it." He shook his head, but his smile told her everything. He might warn her, but there was no way he was changing his mind. She'd pushed him beyond the point of no return.

The fire crackled in the background, but the heat was coming off their bodies. They were a sizzling hot combination. She'd known it from that first stolen kiss.

"Get into bed." He sat up and put her back on her knees.

Her heart stopped. Had she read him wrong? Was he rejecting her again?

"You're turning me down?"

He rose to his feet and helped her stand. He took in her body and licked his lips.

"It's too late for that, sweetheart. You poked the bear one too many times." He turned her around and swatted her bare bottom. "When I'm pressed into your body, you'll be happy to have the mattress instead of the hardwood floor at your back."

She ran to the bed and climbed on top. The covers were rumpled from earlier. She considered covering herself up, but she loved the way he tracked her movements. Loved the way he took in every inch of her like she was one of the maps he studied.

He kicked off his boots and unbuttoned his jeans with the deliberation of a stripper. Every tooth of his zipper clicked in the silence as he pulled the tab down. The denim hit the floor, leaving him in black boxer briefs and nothing else.

Never once had she considered men's underwear sexy, but seeing Tilden with his tawny skin and his arousal bulging against his stomach, all she could think of was how glorious this mountain man was.

"You sure about this?"

With little thought, she let her legs fall open. It was a bold invitation.

"Take off your briefs before you change your mind."

"Couple of things, sweetheart. Are you protected?"

Her body ... yes. Her heart ... not so sure. "IUD."

"I may have a condom in the truck." He looked over his shoulder to the front door.

She laughed at the thought of him running into the chill of the night air nearly naked in search of a condom.

"Any risky behavior?" she asked.

He shook his head. "Clean as a whistle and it's been so long, I'm almost a virgin again." He dropped his briefs and climbed on the bed.

"Same here. We're good." She'd never wanted children, so protecting herself was paramount. This would be her first skin-on-skin experience. If she'd had it her way in the past, she would have had men double glove before the love but with him it was different. He wasn't having sex with her because he thought she could do something for his career. He wasn't interested in her assets, which sat at zero right now. Couldn't care about her connections. All he wanted was her body for a night and she was willing to give it to him.

"You're my first."

He crawled between her legs and hovered over her body. His length twitched against her.

"Being hard as a rock for you, I'm liable to

believe anything you say but I'm having a hard time believing I'm your first anything."

She pushed on his chest with all her might until they toppled over, and she came to rest over him.

"Not my first ever but my first condom-free experience."

He shifted their bodies so she hovered over him. All it would take was a single move and he'd be inside her. She had no problem with a first-time quickie but knowing the man who breathed heavily beneath her, he might come to his senses after their first time.

Instead, she would tease, titillate and torture him until he begged her for release. If this would only happen once, she wanted to make sure he remembered her for always.

With a shift of her hips, she inched him inside of her. The stretch and pull felt wonderful. He filled her in more ways than he'd ever know.

She'd had a few lovers in her time. Not as many as one would think. Contrary to what most would believe, men were intimidated by women like her. The façade of being an "it" girl made for a lonely life.

Once he was inside her, she rolled her hips and relished the moan that reverberated from deep in his chest.

"You're killing me."

"You'll die happy."

She leaned forward and let her hair fall like a curtain. It was just the two of them with the heat of the fire across the room and the inferno of pent-up desire around them.

"Yes, I will." He lifted to meet the thrust of her hips. His hands cupped her bottom to set the pace.

With closed eyes and a look of pain on his face, he shifted them once again until he was on top.

For a man who hadn't had sex in a long time, he wasn't lacking in restraint. She knew each time he was getting close because of the way his jaw hardened, and the telltale tick of his muscles twitching on his cheek.

Each time she got close he'd move. "Not yet, we're doing this together."

"I'm ready."

He chuckled. "Not yet."

She'd never been flipped in so many positions. Hadn't met a man who was so limber. Loved the way his muscles flexed and hardened. Where did he get his staying power?

She was certain the Kama Sutra had nothing left to show her when he pulled out and ran his whiskers down her stomach to settle between her legs.

One touch of his tongue and she was a quivering mess.

What started out as her intent to make him beg had her repeating "Please. Please. Please" — over and over again.

And just as she was falling over the precipice, he moved up her body and plunged deep inside her. There was no coming back from that experience. She fell apart around him.

When he stilled and said her name, she wondered if maybe he wasn't right. This was a bad decision. Had Tilden ruined her for all other men?

CHAPTER SIXTEEN

He snuck out of bed at first light. It was his way. Up with the sun to start his day. He warmed up the shower water and made the coffee. For over an hour he sat on the edge of the bed and stared at her.

Part of him felt like an idiot for being so irresponsible; the other felt like a caveman wanting to pound his chest for claiming his woman. Right out of the gate he knew she'd be great in bed. A simple kiss from her as a stranger sent jolts of awareness arcing through his body. There had been no doubt they'd be like a lit stick of dynamite in bed together.

They'd agreed it would happen only once, but that was thrown out the window as soon as his refractory time was met. A man his age needed some rest in between, but something about Goldie had him so worked up that he was ready as soon as they finished.

Did they spend all night testing out the strength of the furniture in the cabin? Everywhere he looked was filled with a memory. Goldie on the sofa. Goldie on the table. Goldie against the wall. His home and mind were filled with the woman who now slept naked in his bed.

She stirred and opened an eye.

"Good morning." Her hand snaked out from under the cover and rested on his denim clad thigh. "Come back to bed." Her voice was gravelly and sexy.

"It's getting late. I've got work to do."

She rose up, the sheet falling down to expose her breasts.

Immediately, his body reacted. He couldn't seem to get enough of her. He'd have liked to say it was only her body and the pleasures it gave him that made him respond to her, but he didn't like to lie to himself. There was something about her that called to his inner hero. The part of him that wanted to make things right for her.

It would be easy to discount her because she was not his type. She'd proven that by moving into his cabin and staying for weeks. His type was here tonight, gone before morning. He liked her more than he wanted to. Liked her in a way that he'd liked no one else, and it had very little to do with how she set his body on fire.

She rolled over and laid her head in his lap. "Thanks for last night. You took care of me in a way no one else ever has."

Did she mean sexually or was it because he'd opened his cabin to her?

"Thank you for last night. It was ..." What could he say? It was the most amazing night of his life? There was no way he'd give her that much information. "Great. I really had a good time."

She flopped back and pulled the sheet over her body. Damn shame to cover up such beauty. He looked at his watch and considered the time. He'd asked Wes to come out and look at how much pipe needed to be laid to get inside plumbing. Was he doing it for her or for himself? Things were muddled right now. After seeing her in the bathtub last night, he considered how nice it would be to have a shower he didn't need to light a fire for. To have an indoor toilet that could flush. It was a luxury he could have had all this time but he hadn't placed the priority of comfort over his need for information.

"If I get up now, will you walk me to the

bathroom?" Her eyes grew big and a shudder raced through her body.

"Yes, let's get you dressed and then I've got something to tell you."

He rose to pour her a cup of coffee. Whereas she normally hid in the closet to dress, she no longer needed to hide her nakedness from him. He'd seen every inch of her.

Leaning against the counter and sipping his own cup of coffee, he watched as she climbed out of bed. Even from where he stood, her skin looked as soft as it felt. The telltale sign of his desire for her twitched in his pants.

"Are you going to disappear today?" She hopped into a pair of jeans, then picked up his T-shirt that had been discarded on the floor. She tugged it over her head, slipped on her boots and walked to the back door. She reached for the handle but pulled back. "Is it silly that I'm afraid?"

He put his cup down and walked to her, wrapping his arms around her waist and nuzzling his beard into the crook of her neck.

"Not at all. Last night was a traumatic experience for you. Hell, it was a traumatic experience for me." He lifted his head and kissed her gently on the lips. "It was a great lesson as well. We live in the wild. I like to think of myself as a guest in their woods. You have to always be aware of your surroundings."

They walked to the outhouse and he leaned on a nearby tree and waited.

"Don't listen."

He laughed. "Just hurry. It's cold out here." He crossed his arms over his chest. If he was cold in a long-sleeve Henley and a flannel shirt, there was no doubt she'd be chilled to the bone in his short-sleeved cotton tee.

She walked out rubbing hand sanitizer between her hands. "It's sad when your pee lets off steam."

"Come on. Let's get you inside. I've got some exciting news to tell you."

He put his arm around her and led her back into the cabin. He poured her a cup of coffee and pulled out the chair across the table.

"What's this exciting news?" She ran her hand across the smooth wooden surface and smiled.

He knew she was thinking about last night. He closed his eyes and relived that exact moment. God, he loved this table. How they'd swiped the plans and vials of dirt to the floor before he lifted her to the surface. He was certain she'd be bruised from the pounding against the wood, but she didn't seem bothered by anything except the outdoors.

He leaned back in his chair and stared. Not a stitch of makeup on and she was so beautiful.

"How would you like to have a hot bath every night?" He drank his coffee and watched for her reaction.

A smile lifted the corners of her lips. "Are you going to boil water for me and light candles and pour me a glass of wine each evening?" She winked. "That almost sounds like planned seduction, Mr. Cool. I thought last night was a one-time thing."

He leaned forward. "I'm talking about finishing the piping to the house. Getting a big old water heater so you can have your baths." He scooted back his chair and walked to her side of the table. "As for last night ... I wouldn't mind a repeat."

She slid fingers from both hands into his belt loops and tugged him toward her. "You ready now? I'm all about the present. After yesterday, I realize I can be here now and wolf food in the next minute."

He bent over and lifted her like a fireman over his shoulder. Her laughter rang throughout the room.

"How about being my food? I like how you taste." He licked his lips and reached for the button of her jeans. The sound of tires on gravel stopped him short. He stared down at her flushed face. "Raincheck? Looks like Wes is here."

"We're having company?" She bolted off the bed and raced around the room picking up their discarded clothes. There wasn't anywhere to put them, so she opened the closet door and shoved them inside. "You could have said something."

"I did."

Her hands came to her cheeks. "Oh. My. God. We could have been in the middle of ..." She rushed to the bed and wrestled it into submission. As soon as the quilt was tucked over the pillows she walked to the counter and acted as if nothing happened. That was the performer in her. Always ready to take on the role thrown at her.

A knock sounded at the door and Tilden swung it wide open. "Wes, come on in."

Wes wiped his boots on the welcome mat and stepped inside. "Sorry I'm early. I hope I'm not interrupting anything."

Tilden looked at Goldie. "I was just getting ready to eat."

She dropped the empty coffee cup in her hand.

"Coffee?" Red hot heat rushed to Goldie's cheeks.

"Love some. You must be Goldie."

She smiled and lowered her head. "That's me." She poured him a cup of coffee and moved into the living room. "I'd leave you two to yourselves, but there's no place for me to go except outside." She glanced at the door. "And that's not happening."

"Goldie had a run-in with a wolf last night." Tilden cleared his throat. "That's why I thought it might be a good idea to get the plumbing finished."

"No shit. That must have scared the hell out of you."

"It wasn't pleasant," she said.

His builder's eyes moved around the cabin. "This place hasn't changed." Then he looked at Goldie. "Maybe. Can't remember a time when I've ever seen a woman here."

Tilden waved him over to the table. It was no longer the clean slate for lovemaking; his maps and vials had been placed back on top early this morning.

"You spend some time in this place?" Tilden asked.

Wes nodded. "Ray had Tuesday night poker from time to time." He pointed to the walls of books. "Can't remember Ray being bookish."

"That's all me. I built the shelves to house my guilty pleasure."

Wes picked up a vial of soil. "Books, maps and dirt. It's always the quiet ones. I hear you're some sort of scholar."

He shook his head. "Shouldn't believe everything you hear. I used to be a high school history teacher."

Goldie sat up. "You were?"

"What about you, Goldie? Are books your thing too?"

Both men looked at her, but it was Tilden who saw the slight change in her expression. The thinning of her lips and the glazed-over look she got when she took in the bookshelves.

Tilden answered for her. "Goldie believes that a picture is worth a thousand words. Whereas I like to read the words, she'd prefer the movies." He pointed at the phone in her hand. "She doesn't even read her messages but has text to voice talk to her like a personal secretary."

Wes shrugged. "Everyone has their thing. Lydia likes cozy mysteries and bodice ripper romances. I bury my head in architecture magazines." He touched the maps. "What's this all about?"

"Nothing really. Just a bunch of old maps Ray left behind." He saw Goldie's mouth drop open, but she didn't say a word.

"I get it. History buff and all."

"Something like that." He pushed the papers to the side. "What about the piping? I think it's almost to the house. Maybe another fifty feet or so and we can hook up the water and install a big ass tank."

Wes rose from his seat. "Let's have a look." He waved to Goldie. "Good to meet you. See you soon. You're working at the brewhouse on the weekends, right?"

"For now."

Tilden didn't like that answer. For now, meant she was thinking about something different in the future. While Wes might not have noticed the change in tone to her voice, he did.

They walked out the door and he showed Wes where the line ended.

"I didn't know you were still dealing with a pump and an outhouse. We could have fixed this right away."

"Money got in the way, but with Goldie here ... well, I don't want her running to the outhouse in the middle of the night."

"You two a thing?"

Tilden looked over his shoulder. "I'm not sure what we are, but we're something."

"Everything starts with something."

Wes told him he had a couple of guys out of work for the winter that would be happy to bring up the trencher and pave the way for the new piping. If all went according to plan, they could have it finished up and inspected by Friday. Once they agreed on a price, Wes left, and Tilden walked inside to find Goldie sitting at the table looking over his maps.

"Why did you lie to him?"

"What?"

"You told him these maps were Ray's. They're not. You drive to Copper Creek every week to get information on this plot of land. Why?" She pushed the maps away from her and looked up at him. "Why didn't you tell me you were a history teacher?"

He wasn't ready for this conversation. "Because I don't owe you my truth."

She pushed back from the table and fisted her hips. "It's fine for you to tell me to be authentic when you're lying to everyone around you. I thought you were real, but you're worse than my friends. At least I know they're fake. But you ... you made me believe in you, and I have no idea who in the hell you are."

"The difference between you and me is that I never lied to myself. You do that all the time."

"I know exactly who I am. I'm the girl who gave you everything she had left to give last night. Shame on you for taking what you didn't deserve. Shame on me for thinking you did." She picked up her mug of coffee and flung it at him. The handle skimmed his cheek and crashed against the door.

He grabbed his keys and walked out the front.

"You said you wouldn't leave," she yelled after him.

He started his truck and took off toward town. Goldie Sutherland had gotten under his skin and he needed to distance himself.

When he reached the diner, he walked inside and looked around. His normal table was vacant, but he didn't take it.

Doc was seated in the back, corner booth. He was known as the town mentor and Tilden needed advice.

"Mind if I join you?" He stood at the edge of the table and looked over Doc's newspaper.

Doc folded his paper and set it aside. "Have a seat, son. What's on your mind?" He took a deep breath and told him all about Goldie and her social media life. How she had trust issues and how he wasn't sure where she fit in his world, but he knew she fit.

"How much truth does a person need to know? Can't a man have some secrets?"

Doc moved his lips, which made his mustache shift left to right. "You like this woman?"

Tilden rubbed his eyes.

"I do, but I have some reservations."

He had feelings for Goldie, but he wasn't sure how deep they ran. All he knew was that having her in his life was far better than being alone. That even seemed shallow because she was far more than a warm body. She made him laugh. He loved the way her smile could dazzle him. Loved the stories she told about her life as the child of a movie star. Hers wasn't the easy life people would assume. It came with the ever-present eye of the paparazzi. The judgment of the world.

"What's got you worried?"

"She was never able to be herself and that makes me wonder if the woman in my cabin is actually the woman I'm falling for or someone in transition to being her true self?"

Doc laid his gnarled hands on the table. "Aren't we all in transition? No one is their true self. We're all evolving. You can be a role model for Goldie. You've already become someplace safe for her to land. What a gift you can give each other. To grow and mold each other into the best people you can be."

"But what if we've both been dishonest with each other?"

"Straighten it out, son. The truth can never be too late and starting a relationship on truth will give you a solid foundation."

Doc looked down at his half-eaten pancakes. "You want any more advice you'll need to make an appointment. Lovey is waiting for me to take her to Bingo in Copper Creek."

Tilden pulled a twenty from his wallet and set it on the table. "Breakfast is on me, Doc. Thanks for the wisdom."

"Anytime."

Tilden turned around and walked out of the diner. Could he be honest with Goldie about everything? It wasn't so much that someone in his family might have been a murderer but about how he'd kept his known identity secret to the people he liked the best. Eventually, he'd have to come clean to everyone. His mother once told him that being a liar was the worst sin of all because it stole the truth from everyone else. Goldie deserved better. She'd been honest with him. Wasn't it time he was honest with her?

CHAPTER SEVENTEEN

Goldie didn't like the silence. Her life had always been full of noise. If it wasn't the click of the camera, it was something else. Traffic, movie set equipment, her tutor, her phone.

She hated that Tilden left her alone in the cabin. Hated that he lied to her. Hated that he was right about her lying to herself. She flopped onto the bed and pulled the pillow over her head and screamed.

Her mother told her that all good things in life came in threes. Like a story, there was a beginning, a middle, and an end. A good meal started with ingredients, the skill to cook them, and a moment to enjoy. Love started with courtship, a proposal, and a marriage. A fight began with a difference of opinion, an argument, and then the makeup session.

She screamed again into the pillow. When something touched her leg, she dropped the pillow and screamed again, certain the wolf had made it inside the house, and she was about to be its meal.

There was a wolf all right. He had big, dark chocolate eyes and a beard that could make her sing when it was rubbed in the right places.

"Get your coat, we're leaving," his gruff voice demanded. He let his fingers skim down her leg as he walked away.

When he opened the door, a few flakes of snow blew inside.

Her mind reeled. Was he kicking her out?

No, he couldn't be, or he would have told her to get her stuff and leave. He said to get her coat because *they* were leaving.

She rushed to the closet and pulled on the pink felt jacket that was perfect for short jaunts in the outdoors, but not made for an arctic trek. After she shoved her hair into the matching hat, she walked outside and found Tilden leaning against his truck.

How funny was it that only weeks ago she thought he looked like a cross between a convict and a grizzly bear, and today he was the most handsome man she'd ever laid eyes on?

"Where are we going?" She stomped forward, the layer of snow on the ground eating up the sound of her boots. "If you're going to murder me and leave me in the woods, I want to text one of my friends and let them know." She held up her phone and smiled, hoping to get a different expression than narrowed eyes and a frown.

He walked toward her and cupped her cheek. "Honey, I'm your only friend, and I alone will know where I've dumped your body." The corners of his lips twitched until they rose into a smile that lasted only a second. One glorious second.

With his hand on her back, he led her to the passenger side of the truck and helped her into her seat. "Kiss me now because I fear you may not want to after this trip. I need one more taste of your sweet lips." He didn't give her a chance to think about it. He covered her mouth with his and kissed her like it would be their last. It was an angry kiss that somewhat felt heavy with misery. When he pulled away, there was so much sadness in his eyes that she nearly cried.

When he climbed into the driver's seat, she asked again, "Where are we going?"

"We're seeking the truth."

"Whose truth?"

He reached over and held her hand. "Mine, because I haven't been fair to you. A wise man told me that all relationships should start on a solid foundation."

She twisted her body to face him. "Are we in a relationship?" They had agreed that it was one night, but those were cursory words to get the moment started. She wasn't a one-night stand girl. She'd only had one before him and it took a month of hot showers to cleanse that bad decision from her body. Last night was different. It didn't feel like a bad decision. It was perfect in the most imperfect way. Another three. Hot bath. Wine. Amazing sex.

He gave her a quick glance. "I don't know what we are, but I feel like I'm the spider and you're the fly. You're caught in my web. Then again, maybe you're the spider and I'm the fly, and I'm caught in yours. Either way, you should know the truth."

Her heart raced. It was all so cryptic, so cloak and dagger. What could he tell her that needed an immediate trip in a winter storm?

"Have you been to prison?"

He dropped her hand and put it on the steering wheel. "No."

"Why didn't you tell me you were a history teacher?"

He shook his head. "It wasn't relevant, and it would open the conversation to more questions."

"Questions you don't want to answer?"

He gave her a side glance. "Questions I wasn't prepared to answer."

She crossed her arms over her chest. "And now you are?"

He sat with his shoulders stiff, and his eyes forward. His body leaned toward hers when he took a quick turn onto a country road that led into the mountains.

"I'm ready because of you. You deserve to get a glimpse at the full picture."

"Everyone around town says you never talk. Is it because of whatever truth you're going to tell me?"

He let out a breath and his shoulders relaxed. "As a general rule, I'm a quiet man. I don't need much more than a good book and a comfortable chair." He pulled the truck to the edge of a vista. Big flakes of snow floated down around them. When he killed the engine there wasn't a sound except for their breathing. "Look, I don't say much to others because when I'm silent, no one engages. Until I find out the truth about my family, I don't want people asking questions."

"Your family?"

He turned the key halfway so the wipers turned on. "You see that land?" He pointed to the wide-open space in front of them. "Look out as far as you can."

She leaned toward the windshield and squinted to see through the storm. Every once in a while, she'd glimpse a mountain range on the other side of the flat expanse.

"Okay, it's a lot of land. What does it have to do with you?"

"That's the question of the day. I'm about ninety-nine percent sure that my family owned that land. We're talking hundreds, maybe thousands of acres."

If his family owned the land, why was he living in a small cabin without running water? "I don't understand."

He unbuckled his seatbelt and turned toward her. His eyes were shadowed and tired. No doubt because he'd stayed up all night pleasuring her.

"In order to comprehend what I'm dealing with now, you have to go back to the late eighteen-hundreds, when the Coolidges owned this land. They grew wheat and hops and corn. Like Zachariah, they did a bit of bootlegging, except back then, it was legal."

"Is Zachariah a relative?"

His breath sputtered from his lips. "God, I hope not. It's bad enough that I found out Ray is probably related to me. If rumors are true, he's part of a line started when Abby Garrett's grandfather had an affair with my great-great-aunt Virginia, who was already married. I might have to feed myself to the wolves if I found out I was kin to old man Tucker."

"You're saying you're a Coolidge and not a Cool."

"I'm legally a Cool. I don't know when the name change happened, but according to my great-great-grandma Treasure's diary, the family name is Coolidge." He stalled for a minute. "What you really need to know is that my great-great-grandfather Isaiah Coolidge might have murdered Walt Carver over water."

She took that in. Many people had skeletons in their closets. She did. Hell, she didn't even know who her father was. Could have been any leading man, to any lighting guy. Her mom always loved the lighting guys because they had the power to make her look younger.

"You're hiding your true identity because someone who probably died over a hundred years ago murdered someone? Are you insane? You probably have a claim to the land."

"I'm not hiding. I'm just not sharing. This is a small town and people have long memories. Their ancestors still live here. Doc, Agatha, Abby, Wes ... they're all related to the founding fathers. Bea Bennett, who passed as I arrived, was the last owner of the property." He gripped the steering wheel until his knuckles turned white. "I like these people. While it would have been easier early on to tell them who I thought I was, I've come to care for and respect them. I value their friendship, and I don't want to risk what I've built here. I don't want them to judge me."

She couldn't believe what she was hearing. "You don't want them to judge you? Wasn't it you who gave me a hard time for allowing people to judge me? You're no different than me. Hiding under your great-great-grandmother's petticoats is like me hiding behind my lies about my age and my size and my financial position. I fooled everyone for so long that I started to believe my own lies. Can you believe that I had to look at my driver's license to know how old I really was?"

His face turned red. "You and I are nothing alike. You used people to make money, and I refuse to use anyone."

"You're wrong, you're using everyone but it's worse because they don't know it. At least I was transparent about why I did what I did." She put on a fake smile and pointed down. "There was no false message in 'click the link below because I need another Prada bag.' You don't get to talk out both sides of your mouth and condemn me for trying to stay in the spotlight when you refuse to own up to who you are."

"Are you telling me you owned up to who you were?" he asked. The heat of anger rolled in waves between them.

The energy dance in the air was making the hair on her scalp tingle.

"No, but I was trying to become something. I wasn't hiding in a one-room cabin. Poring over maps. I was ..." She thought about where she was going with her thoughts. She nearly sunk in her seat. "You know what ... you and I are exactly alike. Neither one of us is owning who we are. Both of us are doing our best to correct past mistakes, whether they be ours or our ancestors'. You're the pot calling the kettle black."

He looked out at the land in front of him.

A single ray of light broke through the clouds to light up what should have been his land.

"It's not the same. No one in your family killed anyone."

She swallowed hard. "No, but what you're not focusing on is you didn't kill anyone. You can't be responsible for what happened before you."

"Don't you get it? They ran my family out of town. That forever changed the trajectory of our lives. We were no longer landowners. My mom waited tables until she died from an aneurysm and my dad drank himself to death. How different things would have been if my ancestors had worked their land, grown their wheat, sold their moonshine."

"Don't forget that they aren't their ancestors either. You can't change the past, but you can change your future."

"That's exactly what I'm trying to do, but I care about the people of Aspen Cove. I don't want them to hate me."

She understood that all too well. "They can't hate you. Hell, they don't know you. Show them who you are. If they hate you after that, then that's their problem. Wasn't it you who told me to be authentic? Practice what you preach."

CHAPTER EIGHTEEN

Goldie's words ran through Tilden's head all the way home. When they pulled in front of the cabin she jumped out before he could come to a complete stop.

He rushed inside after her. "Come on, Goldie, talk to me."

"I have nothing to say." She discarded her coat and went straight to the kitchen and started to cook. He had no idea what she was throwing together. They'd missed breakfast and it was moving past lunchtime. The sound of the blade hitting the cutting board echoed off the walls.

"You're mad at me."

She scooped up the celery she'd been slicing

and threw it into a pot, then went to murdering an onion.

"I'm disappointed in you."

He'd never seen anyone with knife skills like hers. She'd diced that onion in seconds. Next came a chicken she pulled from the refrigerator and since he hadn't bought it, he knew she must have.

"I'm disappointed in myself. I never meant to hurt you. Never meant to lie to you. I just didn't think it was important."

She stabbed the knife into the cutting board. It stuck, the handle facing up. "What you thought was important was that someone who lived years ago might have murdered someone? I don't care, but it would have been nice to know that the man I slept with was a liar. I let you into my body. Really into my body. No condom. You could have lied about everything."

"I didn't."

She threw her hands into the air. "How would I know?"

She was right. One lie cast a shadow on all the truths he'd told. "You wouldn't, but I'm asking you to trust me."

A ring tone floated through the air. Goldie wiped her hands on a towel and reached inside her back pocket for her phone.

"Hello."

He didn't know who she was talking to. She didn't have regular callers. No one had bothered to phone her since she'd moved into his place. He kind of enjoyed being the only one she could count on and yet he wasn't. If she considered him a liar, then she'd never depend on him again.

"Yes, I'll be right in." She ended the call and tucked her phone back into her pocket. She rushed around the kitchen tossing spices and the chicken into the pot.

"Who was that?" he asked.

"My boss. I need to go to work." She placed the pot on top of the stove. "Put six cups of water in here and let it simmer for several hours. It's chicken soup for your soul." She washed her hands in the bucket of soapy water they kept in the sink before she shrugged on her jacket and left.

Tilden stood there in the middle of his cabin wondering how things had gotten so out of hand.

All it took was one kiss from a beautiful woman to upset his balance. Or maybe, the balance was always skewed but Goldie was shifting it back into place.

He did as he was told and put six cups of water into the pot and turned on the burner. While the soup cooked, he pored over the maps

once more. When he couldn't come up with anything new, he folded up his research and put it
away. Some things were worth fighting for. Some
were not. He'd been obsessed with clearing his
family's name, but what would it matter if he ruined his in the process?

He tucked the most recent soil samples into a
box to mail. These would be the final samples
he'd test. If nothing came out of it then he'd have
to accept that he might never know what
happened.

As the aroma of chicken soup took over, his
thoughts went to Goldie and how much his life
had changed since she'd been there. He often
made breakfast for both of them, but she had
gotten in the habit of throwing something together for lunch or dinner when they didn't head
into town to the diner.

She was quite the culinary master. Not once
did she read a recipe or measure an ingredient.
She did everything by taste and touch. And
Goldie had quite the touch. He closed his eyes
and relived the night before. All the touches and
all the feels. Somehow, they'd gone subdermal
and found their way to his heart.

Once the soup was finished, he let it cool and
put it away for later. He didn't like thinking
about Goldie at the brewhouse without him

there. There were too many single men who thought they could offer her more. But he knew what she needed. She needed to feel valued. Needed to be loved. Needed to trust the people around her to have her best interests at heart. He wasn't sure she'd ever had that. Wasn't it time he showed her she could let go of her past? Let go of her social media obsession and depend on him?

He looked down at his ragged jeans and plaid flannel. How long had it been since he'd dressed for a date?

"Goldie Sutherland ... I'll show you I'm a smart bet." He laughed at himself. Who talked to an empty room?

Digging deep into the back of the drawers below the bed, he found a clean pair of khakis. Hanging in the closet was his favorite Oxford shirt. It was the one he used to wear on test day. Something about it made it feel lucky. Each time he put it on, his class aced the test. Maybe its luck would work for him. Something told him that Goldie would grade everything he did from here on out.

Once dressed, he spritzed on some rarely worn cologne and swiped up the box of samples. He took the back route to the Copper Creek post office and got back to town just before dinner. Knowing the bar didn't serve food and that

Goldie hadn't eaten before she left, he stopped at the diner to get her favorite fried chicken and mashed potato dinner.

"What are you all dolled up for?" Maisey asked.

His cheeks heated. God, it felt like he was getting ready to knock on the door of his first date. "I'm not dolled up."

Maisey walked around him. "Collared shirt and no jeans? For you, that's like wearing a suit and tie."

He laughed. "She was right. No one here knows me."

Maisey pointed to the counter. "Wait there while I give Ben your order." She was back in a second. "You're right. You are the mystery man in town. Tell me something no one knows about Tilden Cool."

This would have been the perfect time to say he was a Coolidge in hiding but one problem was enough to tackle at a time and getting Goldie to trust him was his main objective.

He rubbed his jaw. "One thing you don't know about me is I used to be a high school history teacher."

Maisey put a cup in front of him and filled it with coffee.

"No kidding." She raised a brow. "What happened?"

"Nothing really." He wanted to blurt out the truth, but it would take him hours to explain so he left it at that.

"Glad nothing brought you to Aspen Cove."

"Nothing might have brought me here, but your cooking kept me here."

She shook her head. "Can't boil water on my own. The cooking is all Dalton and Ben."

"Not true. Who cooked when Ben wasn't yours and when Dalton was away?" After living in a small town, he'd heard all the stories. Maisey's son Dalton had been in prison for killing a man. A man that most likely deserved to die. He stepped in to help a woman and the punch he threw to defend her killed her abuser. That was it for Dalton. Six years in a cell for being an upstanding citizen. Ben, on the other hand, had been the town drunk and the love of a good woman set him straight.

She popped him on the head with her order pad. "Shh, I've stayed out of the kitchen for almost two years now. Don't go spoiling it for me."

He buttoned his lip. "Your secret is safe."

She leaned against the counter. "And yours is safe with me."

He laughed. "Oh, it's no secret. I just didn't think it was important information to share."

"Tell that to Louise, whose oldest is struggling with his history lessons. Says the past is already done so it doesn't matter." She turned around and picked up the Styrofoam container that popped up inside the window.

"There might be some wisdom to his thinking. Although when we study the past, we often can forge a better future."

"Had she known you could help you would have been eating for free in exchange for tutoring."

He tucked a few napkins in his pocket and pulled out enough money to pay for the meal and the coffee.

"Tell her I'd be happy to help."

Maisey pushed his money back at him. "I'll tell her I paid for the first session."

He stood and leaned forward to give her a kiss on the cheek.

Ben glanced out the kitchen window. "Don't be poaching on my land, young man. That woman is taken."

He knew by Ben's smile he was teasing.

"No worries there, I've got my own woman. Or I hope I can make her mine. If your fried chicken doesn't do it then nothing will."

Ben laughed and slapped the counter. "Throw in some kisses too. Those always seem to work."

Tilden took his order and walked outside. The snow had stopped but his breath puffed out in clouds of white.

He stood outside of the brewhouse, readying himself to do something he'd never done—beg. He was intent on getting Goldie back in his life. What would it take to earn her trust?

CHAPTER NINETEEN

Goldie was pulling pitchers of beer when Cannon moved behind her to close a few checks on the register. Mike, his one-eyed cat, lay on the top as if he were watching over everything.

"Thanks for coming in, Goldie." The *ka-ching* of the drawer opening and closing only added to the din of drinkers who were catching every bit of football they could get in before the Super Bowl. "Sage isn't feeling well."

She set another full pitcher on the counter and started on the next. Cannon had asked for three.

"I hope she doesn't have the flu or anything."

He smiled when he turned around. "Oh, I think she's got something, but it isn't the flu."

Goldie almost dropped the pitcher. "You think she's pregnant?" That word gave her a chill. Not everyone was cut out to be a mom. She knew she wasn't. She had no maternal instincts and her internal clock had never started ticking. Not that she disliked kids; she'd never been around any. Even when she was one, her life was filled with adults.

He puffed his chest out. "I hope so. We've been practicing a lot." He picked up a pitcher and slid his fingers through several frosted mugs. "Don't tell anyone. She'd kill me."

She set the next pitcher down. "Won't tell a soul. I'm good at secrets." What that meant was she was good at lies. How funny that perspective changed everything. Was something you kept to yourself really a lie?

When she finished at the taps, she topped off the bowls of snack mix. The whole situation with Tilden had been pinging inside her head since she'd left him. She was angry, but it wasn't about him not telling her he was a teacher, or divulging secrets about his family. What she was angry about was he'd chastised her for not being authentic when he was guilty of the same thing.

As if her thoughts summoned him, he walked inside the bar carrying a Styrofoam container. Even from where she stood, she could smell fried chicken.

The end chair always seemed to be waiting for him. No one liked to sit there because it was so far removed from everyone else. It reminded her of the time-out chair in her mom's makeup trailer. It was where she'd sat when she got in trouble. Seemed fitting that he sit there now.

"Evening, Goldie." His deep voice rumbled through her insides, making them twist and turn, but it wasn't pain she was feeling. It was longing.

"Beer?"

He nodded. "Dark."

"Your mood or the beer?" She looked at the box he'd set on the bar.

"The beer." He slid the container toward her. "You didn't have time to eat. I thought I'd bring your favorite."

It was so hard to be mad at him when he was offering fried chicken and mashed potatoes. "I picked up a muffin at the bakery before I came in."

His big hand reached out and pulled the container back to him. He opened it and picked up a leg.

She could hear the crunch of the coating. When the juice ran down his face, she wanted to lean over and lap it up, but she was far too stubborn to give in so easily.

"If you change your mind, there's plenty. Remember the first time we shared this meal?"

How could she forget? Had it only been a few weeks ago?

"You asked for a place to stay." He took another bite, chewed and swallowed. "For a few days."

"I know, I took advantage of you."

He shrugged. "It hasn't been a hardship. I've enjoyed your company."

A man sitting across the room raised his empty mug. She rushed around the bar to get it. "One more?"

"Another round for me and my brothers." He motioned for the three other men sitting at the table to drink up. "I'm Noah, the ugly one there is Ethan and the other two are the twins, Quinn and Bayden."

"Nice to meet you." She stared at the two he called the twins. "Wouldn't have pegged you two as brothers, much less twins."

"Two eggs, two sperm, one mother," Quinn said.

She pointed to herself. "One egg, one mother, not sure about the sperm. I like to pretend I was delivered by the stork or maybe created by a magic spell."

"Believe anything you want," Ethan said, "but never let anyone tell you you're not beautiful."

"Thank you." She glanced over her shoulder toward Tilden, whose eyes tracked her like lasers. She could feel the heat of his stare at her back. "Lager all around?"

The men nodded and went back to their conversation about building. There seemed to be a lot of construction crews in town.

Sage had told her that the town had almost been a ghost town several years ago. Hard to believe now. The only thing that hinted at a downslope in the economy was the vacant dry good store.

She gathered their mugs and got their refills.

"Have a piece of chicken, Goldie. You know you want one." He held up the thigh. It was her favorite piece and he knew it.

"You are so mean. Such a tease."

Cannon walked over and leaned against the counter. "Go take a break and eat your chicken. It will get busier before it slows down."

"I don't want it. I'm not hungry." Her traitorous stomach growled, giving her away.

Cannon looked at them. "What's going on between the two of you?"

She smiled. "Foreplay." She plucked the thigh from Tilden's fingers and rushed toward the back door that led to the alleyway.

Before she made it outside, she heard Cannon tell Tilden that he was in big trouble.

Leaning against the wall, she devoured the thigh in a few bites.

The night was clear and crisp. A million stars were coming to life above her. To pass the time, she pulled out her phone to check her messages. She'd given up checking them daily because people were mean. A daily dose of what they were handing out could make a girl want to jump from the highest bridge. She figured she'd save up all the vitriol for single large doses.

Only this time, they weren't mean. The last time she'd posted was the day she broke down. Under that post, there were thank you messages for getting real. Messages of encouragement. There was one that said she'd make great bear food, but other than that, it was mostly positive. People weren't tired of her, but tired of her approach. They weren't interested in the sponsorships and products, only the truth. Funny how her life had been surrounded with a scream for the truth.

"You want more truth?" She held the camera out as if to take a selfie. "I'm not the same girl you used to see. The false lashes are gone, and the dark roots are growing in." She pointed to her hair. "It's been weeks since I had a manicure." She scanned the building around her. "I have a real job. My life isn't pretty, but it's real and my life."

She caught movement off to her right.

Tilden was walking her way.

"Smile for the camera, Tilden." In an uncharacteristic move, he flipped her off. She'd never seen him do anything like that and it made her laugh.

His pace quickened until he was standing in front of the camera. "You want to kiss up to an audience who doesn't appreciate you or kiss a man who does?"

She turned the camera back to herself. "Gotta go. I've got a better offer."

As soon as her phone was turned off, he pressed her to the brick wall and covered her mouth with his. They didn't come up for air for minutes.

When Tilden pulled away, he wiped the moisture from her lips with his thumb. "I think your break is up."

She inhaled a much needed breath. How

could the man suck the very air from her lungs and along with it the agitation and anger and hurt she'd felt earlier?

"Are you coming back inside?"

He took her hand and pressed it against his arousal. "When things settle down I will."

She lifted on her tiptoes and kissed him again. "Hurry."

He shook his head. "Honey, last night should have taught you something. Hurry is not in my vocabulary."

Her cheeks burned when she came back inside the bar. No doubt they would be some shade of red. She only hoped the patrons thought it was the change in temperature from outside to inside that caused it.

"You know what breaks like that cause?" Cannon wiped down the counter and looked around the bar.

"Stroke?"

"No, babies."

She laughed. "You and I both know what causes babies, and it isn't a stolen kiss in an alleyway."

He lifted his brows. "No? Well dammit, no wonder I can't knock my wife up. We've been doing it all wrong."

"But you just said that—"

236

He lowered his head. "She called and said it was a false alarm."

"I'm sorry."

A smile spread across his face. "While I'd love to be a father, I don't mind practicing more." Tilden walked toward them. "Looks like you guys are enjoying the practice as well."

She swiped the bar towel from his hands. "Oh, we're just beginners."

"Got to start somewhere."

She thought about her mother's theories on three. They had the beginning, was this the middle? Where would it lead? To a life of happiness or the end?

CHAPTER TWENTY

Tilden wondered how it had gotten to Friday already. Maybe it was the long nights of making up with Goldie or the days of helping Wes's men get the water hooked up to the house. With the frozen ground, it was an arduous task, but after tonight, there would no longer be trips to the outhouse and he'd be able to dismantle the outside shower.

"Are you coming to the brewhouse tonight?" She sat on the edge of the bed and put on her shoes.

He rolled to his side and rose on an elbow. The sheet fell from his chest to wrap around his hips. The way she looked at him like he was dessert always got his body going. When he came in for the day, he found Goldie waiting in bed. Only a stupid man would turn her down.

"I can't tonight." He could, but he was hell-bent on making sure when she got home tonight, she'd be able to slide into a hot bubble bath. The only thing that stood between her and bubbles was buying the bubbles.

He hadn't told her the work was finished. Anytime she asked, he silenced her with a kiss. Wouldn't she be surprised when she came home to wine and candles and suds?

"Finish up the soup if you get hungry." She pulled her coat off the back of the chair and shrugged it on.

"Will do." He loved that soup. Couldn't get enough of it and couldn't get enough of her.

He swung his legs over the edge and attempted to get out of bed, but she covered her eyes and yelled, "No! Don't show me what I'm going to miss. You'll make me want to call in sick."

He stood and tugged the sheet with him. With it wrapped like a toga around his body, he headed for her. "Go to work. I'll be waiting here when you get home."

She looked around the single-room cabin.

"Home ... who would have thought? If you'd told me a month ago I'd be living in the woods with a lumberjack, I would have had you checked for sanity."

"History buff, part-time editor and re-searcher. Not a lumberjack." He nuzzled his beard into the crook of her neck. There was one spot that made her knees weak when he kissed there. His tongue slipped out to lick the hollow, and she grabbed for the chair.

"You are a bad man. A terrible man."

He swatted her bottom. "Go to work, and I'll show you how bad I can be when you get home."

After a final kiss, she walked out the door.

How was it that her absence made every-thing seem dull?

The first thing he did was take a shower, in the house. It had been two years since he'd been able to turn a handle and get hot water on de-mand. Luckily for him, the plumbing had been run for drainage. While the shower heated, he stood over the toilet and flushed it a half dozen times. It was like magic to see the water swirl and disappear, and to watch it fill again so he could repeat the process.

Why hadn't he done this for himself? *Priori-ties out of whack.*

When he stepped into the water, he leaned

against the wall and let it flow over his body. The glorious feeling came only second to being with Goldie. He stayed there until the water ran lukewarm.

After tidying up the cabin, he headed into Copper Creek.

He wasn't sure where he and Goldie stood. While they connected just fine in bed, they hadn't really settled their argument. He'd had three days to think about their positions. She would never understand where he came from because she didn't have the murderer stigma attached to her name. He would never understand her obsession with posting her silly videos.

The other day she asked him to film her chopping wood. It was comical to watch her swing and miss, but eventually, he took the ax away from her for fear she'd chop off a limb. He wasn't sure if it would be his or hers.

He went from store to the store picking up all the things he thought she'd like. Flowers. Wine. Chocolate. Lavender scented bubble bath. He figured if he was already in debt for the plumbing he might as well go all in and get everything he imagined Goldie missed from her old life.

At the checkout, he grabbed a half dozen fashion magazines. As much as Goldie tried to blend in, as much as she acclimated to his simple lifestyle, she was a product of her upbringing. She was the daughter of a movie star. A woman once used to designer labels and Michelin Star restaurants. He couldn't get her those things, but he could get her magazines, flowers and running water.

Once home, he got everything ready. As soon as he saw her headlights shine through the front window, he rose from his corner chair and walked to the door. A glance behind him confirmed he was ready. Flowers on the table. A box of chocolate on her pillow. A stack of magazines on the nightstand by the bed.

He squeezed out the front door and met her halfway.

"How was your night?"

"Busy, but I made ninety-seven dollars in tips." She bounced on the balls of her feet.

He knew if she had more energy, she would have left the ground. There was nothing more humbling than homelessness and starvation. He imagined his cabin looked like a castle compared to the box she'd once considered.

"I bet you're exhausted."

She made her way onto the front porch. "What I would do for a bath." She buried her head against his chest. "Is there any way I can persuade you to lug water into the tub for me? I'd even settle for a few inches."

He laughed. "Nope." He bent over and swept her into her arms.

A yelp left her lips. "Okay, it's late and I'm sure you're tired too."

With her in his arms, he kicked open the door and moved inside. "You get a full tub with bubbles and wine and candlelight. I may have misled you."

She squirmed from his arms and slid down his body to her feet. "We have water? Real running water? A toilet that flushes? We can brush our teeth in the bathroom sink?"

"Yep. We've got it all."

"I forgive you for lying." She slid her arms around his neck and wrapped her legs around his waist. "I feel like we've won the Lotto."

"Just wait." He shuffled to the bed and dumped her on the edge. "Get undressed. I'll get the water ready."

She flopped back and spread her arms over the quilt like she was making snow angels. "How did I get so lucky?"

He laughed. "There wasn't anyone else in the diner when you were looking for a groom."

She rose on her elbows. "Not true. There was Doc Parker."

"I think Agatha would have fought you for him."

"She's a force to be reckoned with. I think she could take me."

She giggled and it was fabulous. The sound of her voice did something to him. It made his heart squeeze. Not painfully, but in a way that showed he still had one. It hadn't shriveled up and died from lack of use.

"I'll be right back." He checked his pocket for the lighter and headed for the bathroom. Along with candles and lavender bath foam, he'd bought new towels. They were soft and fluffy and pink. He didn't know what her favorite color was but took a guess given most of her clothes were some shade of the color.

All night long he questioned his desire to please her and all he could come up with was that he liked her, and Goldie added something to his life. Often it was frustration, but at least she kept him on his toes.

The candles were lit, and the tub was filled with hot water and scented bubbles. A glass of white wine sat on the ledge. All that was missing was her.

When he walked into the main living area, she was curled on her side with her knees pulled up to her chest. Tears were running down her cheeks.

He rushed to her. "You okay?"

She palmed the evidence of her crying away. "Yes, I'm more than okay."

He offered his hand and pulled her to her feet. "Tell me what made you cry." He led her into the bathroom.

She let out a suppressed wail when she walked inside. "You got new towels?"

"You're crying because I got new towels?" He pulled her shirt over her head and sat her on the edge of the tub to pull off her shoes.

"They're pink." She started on her jeans as he finished removing her boots.

He cocked his head to the side. "Pink towels make you cry?"

She was laughing and crying at the same time as she climbed into the water. "Oh my God, this is heaven." She sunk low into the water. The suds touched her chin. "Be careful, Mr. Cool. I'm getting the impression you might like me."

He sat on the edge of the tub and handed her the glass of wine he'd poured. "I do like you. Especially when I don't want to strangle you."

She gasped. "Tell me a time when you wanted to squeeze the life out of me."

He rose and walked to the door. "We don't

have enough time." Before he closed it, he leaned back in. "I'll meet you in bed."

He was naked and waiting when she emerged from the bath wrapped in plush terry cloth. Her cheeks were flushed from the heat of the water.

"That was amazing. Can I live here forever?"

He looked around the cabin. "Why would you want to?"

"Because this is where you are."

She dropped the towel and walked toward him. He had to admit that he liked the weight she'd put on. She complained about her clothes getting tight. Had to lie on the bed to button her jeans, but he loved the way the extra weight felt in his hands.

"But it's not where you should be." He knew she deserved more. Sadly, this was all he had to offer.

"You know where I should be? Under your body. Stop talking and get moving."

He tugged her into bed and ravished her body for the next hour.

They lay sated beside each other. Both had a glass of wine and he reached for the magazines.

When he handed them to her, he noticed the way her smile faltered before she pulled it back into place.

"Thank you so much."

"I bought what I thought you'd like." He hated that his voice sounded defeated.

"They're great." She opened the first magazine and thumbed through several pages.

"Good. I figured if you won't read books, maybe magazines will be your thing. At least it will get you off that damn phone of yours."

She chewed her bottom lip and rose to sit beside him. She opened her mouth and closed it several times. It reminded him of a fish out of water.

"You can tell me anything."

Her expression grew serious. "I don't read because ... it takes me a lifetime to get through a page. I can't even imagine what it would take to get through an entire book."

He hadn't considered the reason she was averse to reading. He scooted back and leaned against the headboard and tapped the space beside him. "Talk to me."

"When I was a kid, my mother thought I was dim. She hired tutors for me. I never got good grades. Lord help me when she got the Growing Up with Goldie gig. I couldn't learn my lines to save her or my life. I had an assistant and it was her job to feed me my lines. Back then they didn't know much about dyslexia."

His eyes grew wide. "Is that why you use text to speech?" It all made sense now.

"That's been my savior for years."

"I had students with dyslexia. It isn't a reflection of your intellect."

"Tell that to my mom."

He pulled her into his arms. "Look at what you've done. You're amazing."

"I did the only thing I knew how to do. I pandered to the public."

"You gave people what they wanted and expected. Was there something else you wanted to do?"

She leaned her head against his chest. "Tons of things. I always wanted to be a princess." She giggled. "One time I thought I'd be a chef."

"You are a chef. You could do that. There's a culinary school in town."

She curled into his body. "Lots of reading."

"I can help you."

"Why would you do that?"

He kissed the top of her head. "Because I'm kind of fond of you."

She lifted and smiled. "Just admit it. You like me. Like really like me."

He tossed the magazines he'd bought to the floor. "I might like you a little." He shut off the light. The truth was he liked her a lot. If he were being honest, his like had crossed into something deeper. He wasn't ready to call it love, but when he thought of her his heart beat faster and harder. In his experience, like only involved his manhood. Love involved his heart.

CHAPTER TWENTY-ONE

Whoever said the truth shall set you free wasn't lying. Goldie hadn't felt this free in ages, if ever. She was authentically herself. There was no faking or pretense. She didn't have to wear the latest fashion or eat at the trendiest restaurants to matter.

Tilden had taught her a lesson. He'd taught her to value herself. She thought back to the day she'd followed him to the cabin. Her instincts were to turn around and leave, but she didn't have any place to go so she was forced by circumstances to acclimate to a simpler way of life.

For the first time in her life, she realized how easy life could be. It had always been a struggle because she'd been programmed to thrive on what other people thought of her. It was a way of life. Now she had time to reflect on who she'd been and who she was.

As she thumbed through Treasure's diary, she had a profound respect for the woman who'd traveled by wagon train from the East Coast to Colorado.

Tilden had teased her for days. She hadn't even wanted to look at a book, weeks ago, and now couldn't put this one down. The first time she opened the tattered leather cover she heard her mother's voice tell her she shouldn't bother. It was funny how the messages she was fed as a child still resonated with her as an adult. She believed her mother. "You can't read," she'd told her. "Why torture yourself? Just use your assets. Beauty and a body never let me down." Goldie had memorized several hundred sight words that got her through everyday life. She didn't investigate dyslexia, had no idea there were fonts that were easier to read. She'd taken her mother's word for everything.

Even Treasure's handwriting didn't pose as much of a problem because she wrote in a way that left the first letter of each word larger than the rest. It helped her understand where one word ended and the next began. That was her problem. Everything ran together in a long string of letters. Sometimes they even jumped around the page. Her reading life was like a perpetual word search. Usually, after a page or two, her eyes crossed and her head hurt, but not so with Treasure's story.

On some level, she was a modern-day Treasure. As she read of the family's journey west, Goldie felt a kinship to the woman who'd battled questionable living conditions, wild animals and people who judged her.

She curled into Tilden's chair in the corner and moved through the diary page by page. It was slow going, but she enjoyed every word.

Tilden was outside dismantling the outhouse. While dealing with refuse was never in her life's plan, she offered to help him, but he told her to stay put.

She looked up when the back door to the cabin opened. Flakes of snow stuck to Tilden's dark hair. His cheeks were apple red from the cold.

She rose from his chair and grabbed a towel from the bedroom to dry him off. "You look frozen."

"It's getting colder, and the snow is coming down harder." He took the towel from her hands and dried himself.

"Do you want coffee?" She'd finally figured

out the pot. Her first attempt at making him a cup produced something that resembled tea, the second looked like mud. Another three entered her life. Probably why the saying was, "if at first you don't succeed, try, try again." Or maybe it's why everyone said third times was a charm.

"I'd love a coffee."

She got the grounds ready and giggled with glee when she turned the faucet handle and water came out. It never got old to turn on the water or flush the toilet. The simple things became the big things when life was put into perspective. All week long she'd been vlogging about her thoughts on life and how she'd had it all wrong before.

"Your great-great-grandmother was quite the gossip."

He stripped out of his wet clothes, which halted her progress on the coffee making. Anytime Tilden was naked she was enraptured. The man had a body honed from stone. Once he was clothed again, she sighed and went back to making the perfect cup.

"Where are you at in her diary?"

"The part where that woman who traveled with them to Colorado had a baby that looked exactly like Major Phelps, the wagon master. Treasure said she tried to pass the child off as her late husband's, who'd been eaten by a bear, but the little boy was a redhead with blue eyes. Both of his supposed parents were dark haired and dark eyed."

"Sad that they ran her out of town too." He pulled the chair to the table out and sat down to look over the new sample reports that came back in the mail.

"Shh, don't tell me the ending."

"Says the girl who only likes to see the movie."

"There is no movie. At least not yet, but it would make a good one. There's mystery, intrigue, infidelity, love, loss, and murder in this book. It's a Hollywood blockbuster."

She put a cup of freshly brewed coffee in front of him. "You play with your dirt, and I'll read the next chapter." She called them chapters, but they were periodic entries. Treasure only wrote when something was noteworthy.

He chuckled and tore open the envelope.

She curled back into his chair and opened the diary to the next page. This one wasn't as exciting. Just a chapter about how Ina Carver, Walt's wife, brought over hand-churned butter and honey from a hive they'd knocked from a tree.

If Abby only knew that honey ran deep in

her veins. Tilden had shared that the Carvers were cattle ranchers, and he thought honey bees had been brought in by Abby, but it must have gone back further than her.

"They were friendly at first."

Tilden lifted his head. "Who?"

"Treasure and Ina were friendly. They shared recipes and resources." On the next page was a handwritten recipe for biscuits that Goldie was excited to try.

"That didn't last long."

She got up from the chair and marched into the kitchen, but not without cuffing him upside the head. "You're a breathing spoiler alert."

He shook his head. "You know the ending, so what is there to spoil?"

She picked up the damp towel he'd set on the kitchen counter and chucked it at him. The toss was so on point, it covered his head.

"When you watch a romance, you know the hero and heroine will get together, that's the promise of a romance, but it's all the stuff that happens in the middle that makes it interesting."

"Romance isn't interesting."

She pulled a canister labeled flour down from the shelf. "Says the man who bought me bubble bath and flowers."

He leaned back in his chair. The front legs came off the floor as he shifted back.

"Maybe you smelled bad and the gift was really for me."

"Or ... maybe you like me more than you're willing to admit." She measured out the amounts written in the diary. "Funny how you bullied me into being honest about my life. Pot. Kettle. Black."

She added the rest of the ingredients and began mixing the sticky dough together. She turned on the oven and dropped spoonfuls of the gooey stuff on a baking sheet while it preheated.

Tilden pushed the papers he was looking at aside. "Dammit."

"Nothing new?" She knew he'd been testing soil samples looking for a smoking gun.

"Same stuff. Trace minerals but nothing more. It's starting to look like Isaiah might have killed Walt Carver. If I can't prove he didn't, what's the point?"

She slid the tray into the oven and came to sit across from him. "What was the point initially? What drove you here?"

He picked up his coffee. "I wanted to find out the truth about myself."

She reached over and placed her hand on top

of his. "You are your own truth. You are not your ancestors just as I'm not my mother."

"It's not the same."

She shrugged. "Maybe not, but isn't it funny what people fight over? Let's promise to never fight."

He put his coffee mug down. "That's not reasonable. We're going to fight."

She let go of his hand and slid it back to her side of the table. "Yes, we will, but let's always make up."

He smiled at her. "Making up with you is half the fun. You want to get in a fight now so we can make up later?" He glanced over his shoulder at their bed.

"Okay, let's fight." She knew what she would say wouldn't make him happy, but it had to be said again. "Why don't you ask the people of Aspen Cove what they know? Some of the people who live here have a long history. Surely they could solve the mystery for you."

The timer went off and she pulled the biscuits from the oven. They looked like tiny blocks of cement. She wouldn't call Treasure a master baker, but she imagined things were different years ago. Rather than make them suffer by eating the hockey pucks, she tossed them into the trash bin.

He pushed from the table. "I've told you already, no one knows anything. I've talked to people. They don't know what happened."

"You've talked to them like a man interested in history. It's different when you're looking to vindicate your family. Their memories might get better."

"Nope. What they don't know can't hurt me."

Sometimes, he could be so frustrating. She didn't understand why Tilden wouldn't ask, then again, she got it because one wrong move could change everyone's perception of a person. He was damned if he did and damned if he didn't, but maybe she could help.

"But the lies we tell ourselves can hurt us too."

"I'm not lying to anyone. I'm just not releasing the information I have."

"Oh, is this where you tell me there's a difference? A secret cannot be a lie simply because it's kept?" They'd both been lying to themselves and to each other, but at least she'd attempted to change.

"It will get worse before it gets better," Tilden said. "I'll get more firewood."

She wasn't sure what he was referring to, but in her experience sometimes worse was for the better. If she hadn't hit rock bottom she wouldn't be here now, and something told her here was where she was supposed to be.

As soon as Tilden pulled on his boots and coat and left, she turned the camera to herself.

She'd been sneaking in live broadcasts when she could, showing her audience what life in the wild had been like, and her numbers were growing again. Just this morning a sponsor contacted her about using their outdoor products, but she was resistant to march down that path again, and she'd turned them down. There were other ways to earn a living. She didn't have to sell her soul for ramen anymore.

While she wouldn't vlog for money, she liked the freedom to say what she wanted and ask for what she wanted. Something had changed over the last week. People were coming to her site asking her opinion about life matters, not lipstick, and it felt good to have something beneficial to share. Her numbers were climbing, which meant people were tuning into Getting Real with Goldie. Thinking about exposure, she did another impromptu post.

"I'm living in a town that had a historic feud over water rights. Tilden has been poring over the history for weeks." She beamed a bright smile. "Yes, that's right, my man is a history buff." She patted herself on the back. "I scored a good one, but I have a riddle for you to solve. I've got a bunch of cattle, a diverted creek, a man obsessed with mining his flat land for gold and two families tired of it all. The cattle are dead and so is the man. What killed them?"

CHAPTER TWENTY-TWO

He zipped through the country road that led to his cabin. Outside of wildlife, there was never anyone driving it. He didn't even get mail delivery. Once a week he headed into Copper Creek to pick up whatever mail had come in.

He was excited to get back to Goldie. He'd bought her a gift sure to keep on giving for years to come. She'd finished the diary and he'd seen her pull *Pride and Prejudice* from the shelf several times. She'd sit and stare at the pages for an eternity before she closed it up and put it away. It broke his heart that she'd miss out on the classics, not to mention all the wonderful books that had come out within the last decade.

He looked at the Kindle box on the seat beside him and smiled. She would love it.

When he pulled up to the house, he saw her in the front yard getting ready to swing the ax. Her lips were moving as if she were talking to someone. On a stump in front of her was her phone.

She was paying more attention to it than to what she was doing. Her stance was all wrong. One swing and the forward motion would take her into a tumble. If she wasn't careful, she'd hurt herself. He threw the truck in park and jumped out.

"Dammit Goldie, you're going to kill yourself." He ran to her and pulled the ax from her grip. "What the hell do you think you're doing?"

"I'm showing my fans how to chop wood." She pointed to the phone propped up on the log.

"Why?"

She turned to face him with her fists on her hips.

"Why what?"

"Why don't you end this nonsense?"

"It's who I am. Asking me to give up social media is like asking you to give up reading."

"Why keep pandering to people who don't matter? Do you think they'd care if you cut off your hand?" He shook his head. "They don't give a shit about you. All they care about is watching you make a spectacle of yourself."

"You're wrong. I've found my purpose, and you helped me get here. I'm being honest about things like how hard it is to cut wood to how dry my damn skin gets when the air turns frigid." She turned and smiled for the camera. "Believe it or not, Crisco is a miracle worker on dry skin."

"If you think this is your purpose in life, then you're not as smart as I thought you were."

He saw the hurt in her eyes, but he also saw the anger.

"Why are you being so mean? More bad news? Nothing in the next batch of tests?"

"Lay off, Goldie. This isn't about me. It's about you."

She'd hit a sore spot. He wasn't used to failing at things. His life hadn't been easy growing up, especially after his mother died. When his father started drinking it only got worse. They survived because Tilden had succeeded. He'd found a job mowing lawns when he wasn't old enough to work. Got a job bagging groceries when he turned sixteen. He stuck his head inside books, so he graduated at the top of his class and got a scholarship. When his dad died, he took his savings to bury him and buy his parents a headstone. Nothing had been easy, but he'd done it. His family had been worth the hardship.

"Why isn't it about you? Why do I have to be honest with myself and everyone watching but you get to hide behind your secrets?"

"I'm telling you to stop now."

She shook her head. "No. I'm not going to stop until you come clean." She shifted so she faced the camera. "This is Tilden Cool. He's a teacher turned mountain man. He moved here to Aspen Cove to find out the truth." She laughed. "The truth about a family feud that changed the trajectory of his life. Only when it happened, he wasn't alive. He wouldn't come to be for over a hundred years later."

"Why are you doing this? Why are you always looking for approval from people who don't matter?"

She stood tall and stomped her foot. "Everyone matters, Tilden. Everyone. You. Me." She pointed to her phone. "Them. We all matter. And I'm trying to live my life with purpose and meaning—to be authentic. To show people that they can change. Lord knows I have."

His lips twisted. There was so much he wanted to say. "Have you? All I see is a woman still looking for acceptance from an audience not worthy of her."

"You know what I see? I see a man who's afraid of losing everything he doesn't have. You're a loner without friends trying to hold on to the lie that you have them. You keep the truth of your identity secret because you're ashamed to know that maybe you have a murderer in your family. Let me tell you something. It. Doesn't. Matter. You are not him." She pressed a finger into his chest. "Everyone, meet Tilden Cool, who hails from the family Coolidge. They were like one half of the Hatfields and McCoys. Only it was the Coolidges and the Carvers. They fought over water rights and someone ended up dead. A lot of cattle perished, and a family was run out of town. His family."

Tilden clenched his fists and backed away. He would never hurt a woman, but in that moment, he wanted to strangle her, or at least put her over his knee and teach her a lesson.

"That was not your story to tell." He took another step backward. "How dare you air my dirty laundry to the public? You just used me for profit. All you care about is money, recognition, and fame."

"Not true. I'm not making a dime. Why I cared about you is dumbfounding because you treat me like I'm stupid. Like what I do is worthless." She swiped at the tear running down her cheek. "I thought you were different, but you're just like my mother, who thought as long as I had her agenda as my priority, I was okay." She pointed to the phone. "And you're worse than they could be. At least they're honest. They don't pull punches with their words. It's brutal and painful to hear the truth about yourself, but sometimes it's necessary."

She marched over to the stump and picked up her phone and looked at it. "Don't forget, the truth will often set you free, but that's after it breaks your heart." She ended the live feed.

She stomped into the house with him on her heels.

He leaned against the door jamb and watched her toss her bag on the bed. He wanted to laugh at how ridiculous the situation was. She was living in a one-room cabin and the woman had a Louis Vuitton bag.

"Where are you going?"

"Not sure but it's not your problem." He stepped away from the door, but she held up her hand. "Don't. You don't get to ask questions."

"Bullshit. You became my problem the minute you offered me money to be your husband."

"You said no. Problem solved."

"No, you're wrong. You begged me to let you stay here and I did. Still my problem."

She moved around the room like a ricocheting bullet. She didn't bother to fold her things. Instead, she shoved shirt after shirt into every nook and cranny of the bag. She marched into the bathroom to get her toothbrush. When she came out, she had the lavender bath foam in her hand. She slammed it on the table. "Use this to wash away the smell of the next girl who becomes your problem."

"That's not fair. I was joking."

She looked around the cabin. "It wasn't funny." She hefted her bag over her shoulder. "I guess this is goodbye."

He could see the tears collect in the corners of her eyes. "Don't leave, Goldie."

She sucked in a deep breath. "I have to. I can't live with someone who doesn't see me for who I am."

She walked out the door and he leaned against the porch post and watched her drive away.

"I'm the only one who has seen you," he said before he walked back inside and closed the door.

IT HAD BEEN three days since she'd left him. Three days of sleeping alone. No laughter. No warmth. No awful coffee.

He'd brought in the Kindle and stared at it for the last three days. He debated sending it back, but he couldn't take what he intended away from her. She loved to read. Her damn mother had made her believe she couldn't when all it would have taken was patience and time.

He set the ereader up to use the open dyslexic font and loaded all the classics for her.

News traveled fast in a small town. The last time he was in the bakery, Katie made it a point to tell him Goldie was staying at B's Bed and Breakfast.

He wouldn't admit it to anyone else, but he was relieved to find out she wasn't living with Baxter. Just thinking about how the man had looked at his woman made him break out into a sweat.

What was more surprising was that she'd stayed in town.

He picked up the Kindle and jumped in his truck. He figured he'd grab a bite to eat at the diner and leave the ereader with someone so they could give it to her.

When he walked inside it was busy and his normal table was occupied. He looked around and found Doc sitting in the corner. The old man waved him over.

He wasn't sure if he was ready for whatever Doc had in mind. Wasn't sure if he knew the truth about his identity. Few people paid attention to Goldie's posts, but he knew Sage did and since Sage worked for Doc Parker, the rumors about him had spread.

"Have a seat, son," Doc said as he approached the table.

"Don't want to interrupt." He looked at the folded newspaper.

"What's in there isn't half as interesting as what's in front of me. You hungry?"

Tilden nodded.

Maisey came by to pour them coffee and walked away with his usual order of cakes and sausage.

"You want to start, or you want me to start?" Doc folded his napkin in half. "Better yet, let's play a game."

Tilden knew that Doc would win but he wouldn't take the fun from the old man.

They went back and forth on the Tic Tac Toe game until Tilden lost, as he knew he would.

"You won." Tilden lined up his knife, fork, and spoon. "You always win."

"Do I?"

He gave Doc a look that said, *Don't play dumb with me.*

"The way I see it is it's not about the outcome of the game. It's about two people moving around each other. Life is a game, son, and you need to know how to play nice with others."

"I get that."

He thought about his fight with Goldie. He was still coming from the place that she had no business telling his story, but she was right about a lot of things. He had marginalized what she found passion in. Her life had always been lived under the scrutiny of the public eye. When he told her to be honest with herself, he didn't realize he'd been telling her to lie to herself. By taking away the one thing she'd always done, he was stripping her of an important part of who she was. She was Goldie Sutherland, daughter of Liza and vlogger extraordinaire.

He'd tuned into her vlog since she'd left and found she hadn't posted, but there were at least a thousand posts about their fight. People came at them from both sides. She was right. She made a difference in people's lives if only because she was willing to show her true self. The good, the bad, and the ugly. Another one of her threes, she'd say. He missed her silly take on the world. How she got giddy each time she turned on the taps. How she'd commandeered his chair to read the diary.

"Now listen here, son. I understand you've been looking for some information."

Maisey dropped off their breakfast and dashed away.

"You already told me what you knew."

Doc chuckled. When he laughed everything seemed to shake, including the table.

"Did I? You weren't asking the right questions. What do you really want to know?"

"I want to know if my great-great-grandfather killed Walt Carver."

"Now see ... I don't know that answer, but I can tell you what I think happened."

"You told me already. You thought he poisoned himself being underground all those hours."

"What have you been searching for?"

"Proof."

"Have you found it yet?"

He cut into his pancakes and shook his head. "No, sir. I've taken sample after sample and spent thousands of dollars testing them. I've got nothing."

Doc swallowed his bite and reached over to tap Tilden on the head with his fork. "You're asking the wrong questions."

"Are you going to keep playing games with me, Doc, or are you going to tell me what you think I ought to know?"

The old man sipped his coffee. "I much prefer the game. It teaches you a lesson. Ask the right people the right questions and you might find your answer. Then again, the answer might be gone forever. Does it really matter who killed Walt?"

"It might if you're Abby." He moved his sausage link around the edge of the plate. "She's his kin."

Doc clucked his tongue. "All that woman cares about is her bees. She's not losing sleep over finding out who Walt Carver was. If the rumors are true, he's your kin too by way of a dalliance."

"That might be the most disturbing bit of information I've learned through the whole thing."

"Can't say I'd disagree. Now, do you have a question for me?"

Tilden thought about all the things he could ask Doc. What was the one thing he might know that could solve the mystery? For the last two years, he felt like a character from the book "Holes," except he wasn't searching for gold but the smoking gun.

Right then he had an epiphany. Maybe he was looking for gold.

"Do you know where Walt Carver had set up his mining operation?"

Doc smiled. "Now, son, you're getting somewhere." He took his time chewing his next bite. He sipped his coffee before he said, "Used to play in the old shaft as a kid."

Holy hell, all this time he could have known if he hadn't been too afraid of what people would think of him. Hadn't Goldie told him the same thing? Her words echoed in his thoughts. "You've talked to them like a man interested in history. It's different when you're looking to vindicate your family. Their memories might get better." She was right. He'd been asking the wrong questions to the right people.

Doc offered to drive out to the Carver ranch with him, but after the detailed directions Doc gave him, he was certain he could find it on his own.

"Thanks, Doc."

He held up his hand. "One more thing, son. Remember the truth always lies somewhere in the middle and life is full of compromises."

"I get that."

"I've seen Goldie around town a lot. You should tell her the truth too."

"She knows everything."

"I'm not talking about your past, but about your feelings."

He shook his head. "I don't have any feelings for Goldie."

The old man lifted a bushy brow. "You need to stop lying to yourself."

Tilden chuckled. "I will." He moved out of the booth and took out his wallet.

"Don't forget you lost and you're buying mine too."

What started as a chuckle turned into a full laugh. "Cheaper than therapy."

"I'll send you my bill."

CHAPTER TWENTY-THREE

Every time the bar door opened, she held her breath, hoping it would be Tilden. What would she do if he showed up? Part of her wanted to walk up and slap him silly, but another part wanted to apologize and tell him she loved him. She had no right to broadcast his secrets. She'd learned all too well in her youth that the truth should come straight from the horse's mouth. She'd crossed a line. Couldn't blame him for not coming to the bar when he knew she'd be working.

"Hey, lady." Katie walked in the bar holding a poorly wrapped gift. For a woman who paid attention to the details, the package looked like it had been wrapped by her toddler Sahara.

"What's up?" It wasn't often that Katie came into the bar, though she made it on most karaoke nights because Maisey watched Sahara and Katie loved to sing but she wasn't a drinker, so the bar had no pull for her.

"A very handsome and lonely-looking man dropped this off for you. Said he'd bought it a week ago but still wanted you to have it."

"Tilden?"

Katie smiled and placed the gift on the counter. "He looks miserable. Mind you, I don't know him all that well, but his normally un-friendly demeanor looks worse. Maybe it's time to bury the hatchet."

She thought about the day they had their blowout. "It was a hatchet, or an ax that started all of this."

Katie sighed. "Whatever it was, don't you think it's time to put it in the past?"

She considered the suggestion. "Problem is that Tilden lives in the past. How can you have a future when you're not even in the present?"

Katie slid the package closer to her. "He wrapped it himself."

Goldie laughed. "I wouldn't say it's at the top of his skillset." She picked up the package that had more tape than paper.

"We have to love all of them, not just the

parts that make our hearts squeeze and our bodies melt."

Why did she have to bring up those parts? She craved Tilden like she craved chocolate, only the need was stronger for the man she loved. She hated to admit it, but she loved him. He was a bear of a man with too much pride. Life had dealt him some dirty hands and somehow, he'd come out on top. Each time she thought of him all she could say was he was a kind and honorable man.

"Thank you for this." She picked up the package and brought it to her chest.

"Do the right thing."

She wasn't sure what the right thing was.

She caught Cannon's attention and pointed to the back door to let him know she was taking a break.

She walked into the chill of the night and leaned against the brick wall of the building. She felt the package but couldn't guess at what was inside.

Like a child at Christmas, she tore through the wrapping paper and found a Kindle. On the screen was a yellow sticky note.

I've loaded some books I think you'll enjoy. The font is set to one that should be helpful. You're the most beautiful woman I know, Goldie, but you're smart. Wisdom doesn't come from books. It comes from life. I miss you. Everything about you.

With love,

Tilden

She opened the cover and the book lit up. Just like he said, the font was like a miracle. Why wasn't everything in the world printed like this? It was because the world wasn't inclusive. There would be the haves and have nots. The pretty and the not as pretty. The smart and the intellectually challenged. Nothing about life was black and white. The truth was often found in the gray areas. She pulled the screen to her lips and kissed the note.

"I miss you too. Everything about you."

When she returned to the bar, he was sitting at the end staring at her. There was no time to approach him because the bar was busy, and he already had a beer.

Each time she looked at him her heart ached. Her body craved him. She pulled her camera from her pocket and went live for a few minutes. She panned the bar and zoomed in on him before turning the camera back to her.

"You can love a man, but you have to love yourself more. Not in the self-centered way but in a self-care way. Loving yourself is understanding what's healthy for you. It's kind of like having one piece of cake when you want two. Know your limits. I'm in love with Tilden Cool but is he the single piece of cake I need, or the extra slice I want?"

CHAPTER TWENTY-FOUR

Tilden sat at the bar and watched Goldie. She was golden: everything and everyone seemed to shine in her presence. Even he was a better man when she was around.

"Tilden, it's been a while."

He smiled. "I was here last week."

"I suppose." Sage followed his line of sight. "Have you ever caught her broadcast?"

He didn't want to say he was obsessed with it. That he listened to every post daily just to hear her voice. "I've caught a few."

She nodded to his phone. "You should catch tonight's. It's really moving." She left him, but it was too noisy in the bar to hear what Goldie posted, so he went out back and leaned against the wall.

It was so cold that his breath turned into cloudy puffs on each exhale. Snow had been falling for the last hour but seeing her on the screen warmed him up. He started at the beginning of her blog called Getting Real with Goldie. He never tired of seeing it. He loved where she'd apologized to her fans and gave the lowdown on beauty products. Loved when she told them that true beauty came from within.

In another one, she flashed her driver's license to reveal her true age but claimed she didn't weigh what it said anymore because Tilden liked mac and cheese with bacon. He watched for close to an hour. Her posts were short and to the point. She was keeping it real. Then he saw her post from tonight, and his heart skipped a beat. She loved him despite everything.

Doc was right, he had been lying to himself. To keep the secret of his feelings from her was as bad as a lie. It was time to come clean.

As he turned to walk back into the bar, he walked into her.

"What are you doing out here?" he asked.

"I saw you come out here an hour ago, but

your truck is still parked out front. Are you okay?"

"No, I'm not." He lifted his hands to cup her cheeks. "I haven't been okay since you left the house. Nothing is the same. Nothing is good." He lowered his head. "I found out the truth about everything and it means nothing without you. Dammit, Goldie, I'm less when you're not by my side."

She leaned into his touch. "Not true."

"Yes, it is. Even the annoying squirrels don't come by the house."

Her shoulders shook with laughter. "It's because you're not leaving nuts out for them."

He narrowed his eyes at her. "Didn't I tell you not to feed the wildlife?"

She stepped toward him. "If I listened to you, you'd starve to death."

"Can we start over?"

"All the way over? As in I shake your hand and tell you I'm Goldie Pearl Sutherland, cocktail waitress and vlogger?"

He took a step back. "Hi, Goldie. I've read every one of your posts. You might be the smartest woman I've ever met. I'm Tilden Isaiah Cool but my family name is Coolidge. It's a long story that I'd love to tell you over breakfast."

"Tilden Cool, are you asking me on a date?"

Heat flooded his entire being. It wasn't the kind of heat that came from passion but the heat that came from love.

"I know this great place that serves decent coffee and great pancakes. You may have heard of it. Maisey's Diner at nine tomorrow morning?"

"If I didn't know better, I'd think you like me."

He leaned in so close he could smell her perfume. He put his lips against her ear.

"Get real, Goldie. I love you." He pressed a chaste kiss to her lips. "Tomorrow at nine? Is it a date?"

She giggled. "I'll try to drag myself away from Mr. Darcy."

He took a step back, afraid if he didn't, he'd pull her into his arms and never let go. "I promise a good time."

She cupped his cheek. "You were always that." She blew him a kiss. "See you tomorrow, Tilden."

He turned around and walked away. His life had come full circle. He had a chance to make everything right with Goldie, but she deserved something special. He'd deliver it in true Goldie style.

HE WAS NEVER HAPPIER than when Bowie's black suit fit him like a glove. He hid in the closed bait and tackle shop until he saw Goldie walk into the diner that morning.

"You got it bad." Bowie reached up like a father sending his son off to prom.

"Oh, I do. She's ... she's a pain the ass and yet, she's my pain in the ass."

Bowie laughed. "I said something similar about Katie. The best thing about women like them is life is never boring."

"How do I look?" He picked up his props and stood tall.

"Like a man heading to the gallows."

He was nervous. They'd barely made up. That little kiss outside could hardly be called more than an ice breaker, but if he had learned anything about his time with Goldie it was that she jumped in with both feet.

She'd gone from penthouse to outhouse and never once complained. Everyone could learn something about strength and fortitude from a woman who'd seen the best and the worst of circumstances.

"I'm so damn nervous. I've got nothing to offer her."

Bowie turned him around and pushed him toward the door. "At the end of the day, all we have is our heart to give. Go give her yours."

Tilden shored up his shoulders and walked out the door. Dressed in the black suit Bowie got married in, he marched across the street and entered the diner.

He looked around at the people sitting in the booths. People he'd known for a couple of years. People who liked him when they didn't know who he was and liked him more when they did. Not one person had turned away after his truth came out. In fact, he'd collected enough information about the feuding families to write a book.

He spotted Goldie sitting at his table. She glanced up from her coffee and cocked her head.

Inside his head, he heard, "Lights, camera, action."

He raised five one-dollar bills in his hand. "I need a wife and I need one now." He walked over to her and sat in the very seat she'd sat in the day she showed up in a cloud of white material. "What about you?" He slapped the bills on the table.

She stared at him and then at the ones. "You're offering me five dollars to marry you?"

He reached out to take her hands. "It's all I

got. I maxed out my credit card to put running water into my place."

Her eyes lit up with mischief. "Oh, you've got running water?"

He nodded. "And a water heater."

"Wow." She dropped one of his hands and reached over to touch his tie. "I always thought I was a suit and tie girl but then I met this history teacher, editor, and sometime lumberjack and I grew fond of him."

He reached up and loosened the tie. "Honey, I'll be anything you want me to be as long as you say yes."

She leaned back and sipped her coffee. Her eyes went to the tie and then to the dollar bills on the table.

"I used to think it was about the package, but now I know it's about the people." She plucked up two of the bills. "How about this. I'll say yes if you promise to keep me in books for the next ten years, and you take part in my vlog. I'm told the couple that plays together stays together."

"I'm all about playing together. It's what we do best."

She blushed. "We do, don't we?"

"You ready to go home, Goldie?"

She scooted her chair out. "Yes—"

"Excuse me."

They looked up to find a man in a gray pin-striped suit standing above them.

"Can I help you?" Tilden asked.

"I think it might be the other way around. I'm here to help you. That is if you're Tilden Cool."

"I am."

The man asked for some form of identification and when Tilden gave him his driver's license, he pulled a pink envelope from his pocket.

"We've been looking for you for over two years."

Tilden stared at the stationery. "I've been here."

The suited man laughed. "Imagine that." He pivoted on his loafers and walked out the door.

"What do you think that is?"

Tilden's hands shook. "I have a feeling this will change our lives."

She placed her hand over the envelope. "Then don't open it. I don't want anything to change. I want to bask in the glory that I took two dollars to be your wife."

"You should have asked for more."

She moved her chair so she sat beside him. "I would have taken less."

They stared at the stationery. "Not opening it is like keeping a secret," he said.

She let out a heavy sigh. "You're right." She pulled out her phone. "Let's get real."

He tore into the envelope to find a handwritten letter on the top.

If you're reading this, it's because you're a Coolidge. You come from a line of amazing people. Over the years you may have heard lots of stories about your family. Their history is quite a tragedy. It never sat right with me that a founding family could be run out of town by the very people who begged them to stay.

Yes, that's right. The Coolidges had their hearts set on the fertile soils in California but the Parkers, Carvers, Guilds and the Bennetts asked them to stay. While they held different last names, they were a family.

The last thing I did was have a surveyor scour the land because I knew the truth was in the gold mine. Enclosed is the report and the deed to the land. I can't make up for everything, but I can right a wrong. You might ask why I felt compelled when my family's name wasn't involved? Because this is Aspen Cove and we're family. Families fight and quarrel, but eventually, they make up. Make your family proud and do what's right for the land.

With love,
Bea Bennett

"Who is Bea Bennett?" Goldie asked.

"I've been told she's a saint."

He looked through the reports and found the same things he'd done. The soil test he had overnighted showed heavy lead and cyanide from the leaching materials Walt used in trying to pull gold from the land. When they'd diverted the water, it flooded his mine. When the pond had bubbled up to the surface, it was full of the toxins that killed Walt and his cattle.

"They didn't do it." Goldie jumped out of her chair and climbed into Tilden's lap. "Your family didn't do it."

"No, they didn't." He pointed to the land deed in front of them. "You know what this means?"

"You're rich?"

He laughed. "Nope, but we have resources and we can build a house on the prairie where there aren't as many wild animals to eat you." He nuzzled his beard into the crook of her neck.

She laughed and plucked up the last three dollars from the table. "Now you can afford more, but I'm not moving out of my cabin. It's got everything I need because it's got you."

Maisey walked over. "You kids want anything?"

Tilden looked up. "Just the check, Maisey. Goldie and I are heading home to play."

CHAPTER TWENTY-FIVE

Three months later.

"We don't need a bigger house." Goldie stood on the sagging porch and watched the big equipment level the soil next to the cabin.

"Yes, we do. We've got friends I'd like to invite over to dinner, and I don't want them in our bedroom when they eat."

"You promise to keep the cabin exactly as it is?" She'd grown attached to the place. It was the last place she would have thought she'd feel comfortable in, but it was the only place that felt like home.

"I'm not changing a thing. It can be what it is." He pulled her to him and wrapped his arms around her waist. "It's where I fell in love with you. I'd never destroy that."

She could hardly believe how much their lives had changed. How one post had transformed everything for them. While Tilden had found out the truth before he received Bea's letter, her report only strengthened his case. A case he didn't need to make in order to belong in Aspen Cove.

Once the title was transferred into his name, he took Goldie over to Abby's house to meet her. She was kin by an affair but family, nonetheless.

They sat over a pitcher of iced tea and talked about bees and honey. She asked what he planned to do with the land but Tilden wasn't certain.

On their way back to the truck, Abby told them that whatever they did it was fine with her.

"Tell me again what kind of house we're building?"

Tilden took her by the hand and walked her toward the plot of land that had been cleared of trees. "It's a green house. Not the type that grows plants, but the type that leaves a smaller footprint on the land."

"You're doing that because you feel guilty that you leased all those acres to Cade Mosier."

Before she knew it, she was swept into his

arms and he was rushing back to the cabin. "You're way too smart for your own good."

They'd made it to the porch when Abby Garrett's truck screeched to a halt in front of them.

She jumped out and raced toward them like an angry hive of bees.

"How could you?" she screamed. "He's destroying my hives."

Tilden looked at her and then at Abby. She could see that part of him wanted to laugh by the twitch of his lips and part of him wanted to hide by the way he leaned toward the door.

Goldie squirmed out of his arms.

She lifted onto her tiptoes and kissed him. "You're up, Mr. McCoy. Time to calm down Ms. Hatfield. I'll be inside waiting for you."

It would seem like another battle was ready to begin, but this time it was between the Mosiers and Garretts and Goldie was putting her money on Abby.

Up next is One Hundred Regrets

GET A FREE BOOK.

Go to www.authorkellycollins.com

ABOUT THE AUTHOR

International bestselling author of more than thirty novels, Kelly Collins writes with the intention of keeping love alive. Always a romantic, she blends real-life events with her vivid imagination to create characters and stories that lovers of contemporary romance, new adult, and romantic suspense will return to again and again.

For More Information
www.authorkellycollins.com
kelly@authorkellycollins.com

Made in the USA
Monee, IL
24 June 2023

37167421R00168